SICK TO DEATH

SICK TO DEATH

DOUGLAS CLARK

PERENNIAL LIBRARY

Harper & Row, Publishers

New York, Cambridge, Philadelphia, San Francisco
London, Mexico City, São Paulo, Sydney

A hardcover edition of this book was published by Stein and Day, Publishers. It is here reprinted by arrangement with John Farquharson Ltd.

First PERENNIAL LIBRARY edition published 1983.

LIBRARY OF CONGRESS CATALOG CARD NUMBER: 83-47582

ISBN: 0-06-080676-1

83 84 85 86 87 10 9 8 7 6 5 4 3 2 1

For Jim Hotchen,
whose knowledge of drugs—
like his willingness to help—
is apparently limitless.

Detective Chief Inspector Masters and Detective Inspector Green were not on speaking terms. They rarely were. The pleasure that each one took in his job was soured by the knowledge that in all major cases it was now accepted that they were paired to work in tandem. Paradoxically, they were a successful team. Know-alls, speculating on their success, attributed it to the fact that each set out to beat the other at every turn. Inevitably, it was said, they were both kept so much on their toes by this exercise that they exerted maximum effort at all times: the basic ingredient of success.

The lovely June morning had not made either of them better disposed towards the other. When the Chief Superintendent had given Masters the warning order for a murder investigation, Masters had not, himself, alerted Green. He had told Sergeant Hill to do it. When Green arrived at Masters' office, the Chief Inspector had already gone for his briefing, while Hill was absent, helping Sergeant Brant to load the Vauxhall with the bags: the travelling laboratory, photographic and other impedimenta of a murder inquiry. So Green was unwelcomed and alone. Left to savour the bitter taste of being summoned by a younger man to a more palatial office than his own to receive orders. He didn't like it. And he didn't like Masters. He wandered around. Sneered inwardly at the cream alpaca jacket Masters kept for hot weather wear but which was now hanging, immaculately ironed, on the coat stand, neighboured by Masters' hand-made showerproof with a removable, bright red, half-lining. Green judged a policeman's efficiency by the length of time he'd worn regulation boots; and for Masters, that time had been short. The minimum. Green's opinion of Masters' ability was similarly curtailed.

Green stopped by the desk. Masters' chair was the biggest the Ministry could provide. And because it was bigger, it was more opulent. Green felt a twinge of envy. Masters, he thought, could get away with anything. Uncharitably, Green supposed that was what happened when a copper had his name printed on his shoe soles.

Green picked up a journal from the desk. Masters' professional background reading. He glanced at an article that said unsolved crime was on the increase because the police were not making enough use of forensic facilities. Green snorted and flung the book down. To him, police routine was all-important. The expert witness was anathema. Somebody who'd go into court and swear black was Bombay tartan if the fee was big enough. He'd no time for semantics—or, as he put it, word-juggling—in court, either. He'd been rattled more than once by defence counsel: made to lose his discreet control by some clever Q.C. who, lacking a case, had wanted to make the police look like lying humbugs. It made Green feel sick with life. For him, once a very happy policeman, his lot since teaming up with Masters was becoming distinctly unhappy. He decided he really would apply for his transfer to a division.

Masters came in, carrying a postcard-size photograph. Without a word he handed it to Green. A girl in a tennis dress that looked as if it might be a Tinling model. Simply cut, the unembroidered purity of its line showed off the pretty figure so elegantly that though still girlish, it looked provocatively mature. Her legs were long and firm with erotically inviting thighs. She was smiling. Obviously happy. A few strands of fair hair had fallen across her eyes, but did nothing to diminish the youthful beauty and freshness of the face. Green studied it for a moment and then handed it back. 'Murdered?' he asked.

2

'A lot of people seem to think so. Including a coroner, the Gloucester police and her doctor.'

'Poor kid. How old? Twenty?'

'Twenty-two. Sally Bowker.'

The thought of the tragedy of this girl seemed to be opening up a channel of communication between them. 'What did she die of?' Green inquired.

'A diabetic coma.'

Green stared for a moment. Still faintly hostile. 'You just said she was murdered. Diabetic coma's ... well, it's natural causes.'

'Not if it's induced.'

'And what does that mean exactly?'

'Brought on unnaturally.'

'How can they tell it was brought on?'

'I'll explain in the car,' Masters said. 'Hill and Brant had better hear.'

'So we're going to Gloucester?'

Masters nodded and took back the photograph.

'It's just the time of year for a run in the country,' Green said. Masters picked up his briefcase and showerproof and followed Green out. They went down, and out to the car in another period of silence. Masters let Green take the near-side back seat because that was where the Inspector felt safest. Brant was in the driving seat; Hill beside him.

'Make for Reading,' Masters instructed. 'Then take the Wantage road. I want to see Streatley, Faringdon and Lechlade. We'll lunch at the riverside pub near the bridge there. The Trout.'

Brant manoeuvred them through London, staying north of the river till Hampton Court bridge. He made good time. The mid-morning traffic was fairly light after the turning up through Virginia Water. Green, by this time slightly less apprehensive than in heavy traffic, asked, 'Now what about this diabetic coma?'

3

'As I understand it,' Masters said, 'although Sally Bowker was diabetic, she was perfectly fit otherwise.'

'That's stretching it a bit. Permanently on the needle and perfectly fit.'

'She's on insulin, remember. Not pot. You saw her photograph.'

'I'll admit what I saw looked O.K. Couldn't wish for anything better. But all those injections two or three times a day! Even though they are only insulin.'

'I can only repeat what I've been told. These days diabetics can be carefully balanced and controlled to keep their disability in check. And evidently when that's achieved, they can live a pretty normal life. Sally Bowker's doctor was so sure she was fit that when he was called to her flat on Monday night and found she'd died in a coma he immediately suspected something out of the ordinary.'

'So he told the local police.'

'And he had the bottle of insulin beside her bed checked.'

'Ah! Hanky-panky?'

Masters took out a brassy new tin of Warlock Flake before replying. As he broke the seal he said, 'It would appear so.'

'Meaning what? That somebody had changed the contents?'

'Nobody is quite sure, but they think not.'

'Slipped in a dollop of some foreign liquid? Water even? That would play havoc with a diabetic, wouldn't it?'

Masters rubbed a fill of Warlock Flake in the palm of one hand with the heel of the other. His empty pipe was gripped between his teeth as he spoke. 'All we know is the insulin in that bottle was useless but not toxic. And that amounts to the same thing with a diabetic. But it was one

4

of a fresh supply she got on prescription last Saturday morning.'

'The chemist she got them from will have some explaining to do.'

'He's already done it. To the coroner yesterday afternoon. He supplied Sally Bowker with four ten mil phials, packed just as they came from the manufacturer. The other three he gave her have been tested, and so have the rest of his particular consignment. They're all perfect. The manufacturers had a research man present at the inquest and he reported that the rest of the batch has been analysed and found to be in good condition.'

Green lit a Kensitas for himself and tossed one over to Hill. Then he said, 'I suppose the bottle we're concerned with had an extruded rubber cap stretched over the neck, and nobody could remove it and replace it without it being as obvious as a pig in a hen run.'

'Quite right. The cap hadn't been tampered with. There was only one puncture in it through which, presumably, Sally Bowker had withdrawn one syringe full on Saturday night. Anyhow, they think so, because the amount missing from the bottle was equal to the number of units of insulin she was supposed to use at each injection.'

Hill half turned in his seat. 'I don't know much about injections,' he said, 'but I'd have thought it would be easy to empty and refill a bottle with a syringe through one hole.'

'We'll probably have to get you to put your theory to the test,' Masters answered. 'But until we know more, further speculation won't get us very far.'

They drove on in silence. Just past Pangbourne, where a stretch of the river opened out close to the road, a motor cruiser was coming downstream, mirrored in water without a ripple, but dotted with tiny splashes here and there as insects alighted or fish rose to the surface. Masters

5

watched with envy. Stillness, peace and pleasure. No murder. The craft had a blue hull and white upperworks. A man was steering: on the cabin top an attractive girl in a yellow bikini, Mexican straw hat and sun glasses. She was stretched out soaking up the sun. She epitomized relaxation for Masters. For Hill she meant other things. He said, 'Just look at that. I could do with taking her down the river myself. It wouldn't take me long to become expert at berthing that little beauty.'

'You haven't seen the photograph of Sally Bowker,' Green said.

Masters was so surprised at the rebuke implied in this remark that without being asked he took the picture from his pocket and handed it to Hill. The sergeant looked at it for a moment, then asked: 'Somebody did away with that bit of capurtle? I don't believe it. No man would be that daft.'

'I don't like it either,' Green said.

Masters grunted and relit his pipe. Green went on: 'I don't like the thought of that lass getting the chop, and I like it even less because it's a medical problem. Medicine's not up our alley. We're going to be hard pushed to pin this on anybody. And that's a pity because I want to get the bastard who did it.'

'Don't be frightened of it,' Masters said. 'We can't afford to be. From the outset we've got to keep it simple. If anybody utters as much as one word we don't understand, we ask for an explanation immediately. If we do that we'll stand a better chance of cutting this business down to size.'

They went along in silence for a few moments. Hill broke it. 'Starveall Farm. Somebody with a sense of humour.' He got no reaction. The road started to rise and dip with the hills. There was little traffic. The sun grew hotter and the tar softer. At Masters' request Brant opened the ventilators. Wantage came up fast and went past slowly as they crawled through the market place.

When they were back in open country again Brant said, 'I've only known one diabetic, and he told me that even ordinary doctors don't know a lot about it.'

'That's my impression, too,' Masters answered. 'It's fairly usual for general practitioners, once they've diagnosed diabetes, to refer the patient straight away to a consultant diabetitian at a hospital or a clinic.'

'Then why was Sally Bowker's ordinary doctor prescribing for her?' Green asked.

'What happens usually, I think, is that the new diabetic goes to the clinic and it's there that all the tests are done and the right initial treatment decided on. You'll remember I said the patients were balanced or controlled? When that's achieved, the patient goes back to his family doctor, who's been told by the clinic what prescription to give him. And this is what the G.P. does in these cases. Prescribes for his patient and keeps an eye on him between visits to the diabetic clinic every three or four months. If a change in medicine or doses of insulin is needed, the clinic makes the adjustments when the time comes.'

'Sounds reasonable,' Green commented. 'But I still think that if the ordinary quacks don't know all that much about diabetes, we're going to find it as hard as little nuts to get to grips.'

Masters didn't reply. Brant slowed to turn right handed over a bridge and slip gently from Berkshire into Gloucestershire. A dozen yards inside the new county he brought the Vauxhall to rest outside the Trout Inn. Masters clambered out, saying, 'I've heard that every table in this place is booked for lunch and dinner weeks in advance. So prepare yourselves for a refusal.' He led the way into the cool interior of the old Cotswold Stone house. They were in luck's way. After a pint of Worthington on the smooth lawn running down to the river they were called to a table and a lunch that kept even Green appreciatively free from odious comparisons with police canteens.

By two o'clock they had skirted Cirencester, leaving it on their right, and were big-dippering along the old Roman way, straight as a Chinaman's pigtail for sixteen miles before turning at Birdlip, where Masters ordered Brant to pull in so that they could all enjoy the view over the city. Then on and down, winding between tall trees in low gear to start the last few miles into Gloucester. At the crossroads in the centre of the city they stopped to ask the way to the station.

Chief Superintendent Hook received them in his office. He was a large, florid man, with a neat moustache that seemed too small for his face. The heat wasn't helping him. He had his jacket off and his sleeves rolled up above the elbows. In one hand he held a wet ball of handkerchief with which, from time to time, he mopped his brow, his bald patch, and the back of his neck. His shirt showed sweat patches under the arms and round the collar, and a great forward thrust in front over the tops of his trousers. His grip as he shook hands was firm but moist. When Hook turned to greet Green and the sergeants, Masters surreptitiously wiped his own palm on his handkerchief.

Hook, labouring under full steam, drew up chairs for them. His charm, a surprising gentleness of manner, was enhanced by the soft, almost Welsh inflexion in his voice. 'I'm mighty glad you've come. And so quickly. Curious case, this is. Not one I care for at all.'

Masters said bluntly, 'Why?'

Hook stared at him for a moment. Then he said, 'Because I don't understand what's going on and because I knew Sally Bowker . . . well, shall we say I really know her father and mother, but I knew her as well.'

'So you are involved personally?'

'Yes. But I'm personally involved in all crime that takes place here, because I was born and bred in this city and know practically every other person in it.'

'That's not what I meant, sir.'

'I know. You're suggesting that my judgment may be clouded because the pretty daughter of an acquaintance of mine is the victim. You're right. I make a habit of walking round Gloucester in my uniform, carrying stick and gloves, to see and be seen. Every day I walk round about the cross in the city centre, and then out a bit to one of the more domestic areas, across the park, round the schools, near the factories—even into the swimming baths. Most people, including the kids, know me. Some of them speak. Some of them look a bit apprehensive at times. We've a large coloured community. They see me and, I think, realize that though I represent the law, I can go among *them* without causing them the least concern if they've given *me* no trouble. You get my point?'

'I do, sir. It seems an admirable habit. An extension of the bobby on the beat. And I can see it doing nothing but good for relations between the police and the public and—as a bonus—for your own health. A constitutional every day is what the doctors order, isn't it? But chiefly I'm impressed that you can make the time to be out and about so much. It says a lot for your administration that you can leave your desk and other duties so regularly.'

Hook waved a disclaiming hand. 'I'm as proud of the way I run things as the next man. But that aside, what I was going to say was that though I'm widely recognized and greeted pretty often by the public, I never enjoyed my jaunts as much as I did on the days when I saw Sally Bowker.'

Green coughed. Hook glanced at him and said: 'I know what you're thinking. A man of my age on the look out for a lovely young lass puts me in the dirty-old-man class. Well,

9

have it that way if you like. But I'll still confess that seeing and passing the time of day with a vivacious, pretty young thing like her was a real tonic to me. And there's a lot of others round here who feel the same way. She skipped along like a kid, you know. Always had a bag on a long strap over her shoulder and swung it as she went, dodging through the crowds. Head high, laughing. I can tell you it wasn't only men who'd turn to look at her. Women, too. She'd a flair for dress. Always simple clothes, but I reckon she'd have looked well in a coal sack with a smudge of slack on her face. I do. Honest.'

'We've seen a picture of her,' Green said.

'Then you'll know.'

'And you're amazed that anybody could kill—even harm—a girl like that?' Masters asked.

'I am that. Apart from me knowing her father, I mean. If I'd never met Donald Bowker, or if Sally hadn't known me from David of the White Rock, I'd still have been nonplussed. Aye, and more than that.'

Masters said, 'You've told us a lot, sir. And it's all useful. Would you care to go a bit further and give us a verbal picture of everything you knew about Miss Bowker? I always find it a great help to know as much as possible about a victim, what she did for a living, her environment, her family, friends, and so on.'

Hook offered him a cigarette. 'I've heard how you work. That's why I've been running on so much.' Masters refused the cigarette and took out his pipe. Hook went on: 'I'll send for a pot of tea—unless you'd like cold squash or something? No? Right.' He spoke into the house phone. He put it down and looked up. 'I'll talk all night if it'll help, but I must have a spot of lubrication. Incidentally, while we're waiting, I might as well tell you we've booked you in at the Bristol in Southgate. It's an old inn not far from here, and it's comfortably near the hospital if you want to chat to the staff of the diabetic clinic there.'

Masters thanked him. The tea was brought in by a W.P.C. who poured out before leaving. As Hook stirred his tea—Masters noted he did it widdershins—he said, 'Donald Bowker's pretty well britched. He farms in a biggish way and runs a light-engineering works. Makes agricultural machinery, mostly. You can see it standing outside his factory all orange and blue.'

Masters said, 'I must interrupt you, sir, because there's a point I'm not quite clear about. If her father is still alive . . .'

'Mother, too. Nice-looking woman.'

'Quite. Then why had Miss Bowker a bachelor flat? A girl who needed frequent medical attention would surely have been better living with her people, who could have given her help and cared for her. Especially if they live close by.'

'Ah! Well, that's it, you see. They don't live close by any more. You came in from the east, didn't you? Yes? In that case you probably saw signposts for places called Brockworth and Hucclecote—on your right as you come in. Gloucester's beginning to sprawl, like everywhere else. Housing estates and shopping centres. All going up in these places outside. And roads, too. Motorways and feed roads. A few hundred yards north, and parallel to the road you used, they've built another great racing-track of a thing, cutting straight across good grazing and agricultural land. Donald Bowker used to farm there. Dairy farm. But some years ago, as I told you, he'd opened up his light-engineering business over near Evesham. When these roads started coming, carving up his land and running past his doorstep, he decided to sell up here and take another farm near his works. So he's been gone the best part of three years now.'

'Leaving his daughter behind.'

Hook nodded and sipped his tea. 'She was a visualizer or designer or whatever they call themselves these days. Sally and another two young lasses had a bit of a bright idea. They found it wasn't so easy getting jobs, because there seem to be more of these so-called artists sculling around these days than there are places for them to fill. So they decided to set up their own little firm and concentrate on window dressing.'

'On what?' Green asked. 'D'you mean to say that shops pay outsiders to put goods in windows?'

'Apparently,' Hook said. 'And not only shops. There's a raft of exhibitions taking place all the time, and people who don't employ their own exhibition managers but who want to take a stand have to get somebody to tart things up for them. But by and large it was shop windows. You know the sort of thing. Spring fashions with banks of plastic daffodils. Winter coats with polystyrene snowmen. Sandals on pebble beaches and highly coloured price tickets stuck on the windows.'

'We see it often enough in London,' Masters said. 'Girls wearing slacks and paddling about in their stocking feet putting model dresses on dummies. But in Gloucester . . .'

'There's enough big shops in Gloucester and Cheltenham to keep all the window dressers in the world busy. Take a look while you're in these parts. Walk down Cheltenham Promenade sometime.'

'I'll take your word for it.' Masters was not a shopping man—unless visits to his tailor and frequent calls on his tobacconist counted.

Hook went on. 'These girls set out to provide a real service. They didn't only dress windows, they designed the displays, and one of them actually used to make and paint the bits and bobs they used. The people who engaged them used to leave the whole thing to them. It took a month or two to get the job off the ground, but I think Donald Bowker chipped in to see they didn't starve. And once the idea caught on! Well, I reckon you could see those girls' handiwork in scores of shops. Not only the really big ones, either. Some of the middling-sized places, too. There's one baby-wear shop not far from here that Sally and her friends did in the middle of last week. It'd do your heart good to see it. They've laid out a whole house and garden with every room showing the effect a baby has on each. They've even got nappies on a line with a concealed fan to blow them about. Wonderful!'

Masters relit his pipe. 'So Miss Bowker stayed in Gloucester in a bachelor flat. In the same block as her business colleagues?'

'No. The other two live in Cheltenham. Sally used to be there, too, until she became engaged to Brian Dent. He lives here, in Gloucester, with his parents, so she moved to be near him. I don't think that was the only reason, though. She was, basically, a Gloucester girl, and the flat she shared with the other two in Cheltenham wasn't really big enough for three. So when these bachelor flats went up in Gloucester, she took one. She told me some time ago it was a good arrangement. She was on the spot for the work at this end, while the other two did Cheltenham and looked after the studio which they'd been able to set up in the flat there after she moved out.'

'What's the name of her firm? And her partners' names, too, please?'

'They call themselves *Show Off*. The other girls are Winifred Bracegirdle and Clara Breese. They were known around about as the three Bs.'

'Good. Now, sir. Miss Bowker was diabetic, she was engaged . . .'

'Wait a bit. She wasn't diabetic when she first got engaged to young Dent.'

'No?'

'No. She's only been diabetic six or eight months. She was engaged a year ago.'

Masters looked thoughtful. 'There was no question of breaking off the engagement?'

Hook was very definite. 'None whatever. The wedding was postponed a bit, perhaps. That I don't really know. I heard she was originally to be married this month, but be that as it may, it was definitely arranged for this September. Preparations were well in hand.'

'Thank you. Now just one or two minor points. Who and what is Brian Dent?'

'He's the son of Harry Dent of Dent and Blackett. They're architects, surveyors, auctioneers, house agents, insurance agents, and everything you can think of. They sell farms, animals, houses . . . the lot.'

'Wealthy?'

Hook grimaced. 'Did you ever know one in that line that wasn't? And they're in a big way. The biggest for miles around.'

'And what is Brian?'

'He's a qualified architect and surveyor. He took Blackett's place when Blackett died. Harry Dent is the auctioneer of the business. A bit of a bluff old sinner. Better at knocking down furniture in the corn exchange than anything else. But not too bad if you can put up with old blowhards like him. Brian's very different. A nice lad. Sally couldn't have picked herself a better.'

'Where do they live?'

Hook gave Masters the address.

'Now, sir, Miss Bowker's doctor? Who's he?'

'Neville Sisson. He lives fairly close by here. Near the library and museum. Got a tumbledown old house. He's youngish, but he's good. Sally was in luck's way with him because he knows a good deal about diabetes. I spoke to him about it once. He told me that the country's pretty short of full time diabetitians—like most things—and so diabetic patients in many hospitals are the responsibility of the consultant physicians. Well, you know how they're fixed. They have to offload a good deal of practical work on to their registrars. And that's what Sisson was. A registrar before he entered practice. He used to run a diabetic clinic twice a week. He still helps at one of our hospitals here. So Sally was in experienced hands.'

Masters said, 'If it was Sisson who refused the death certificate, it shows he knew what he was about.'

Hook helped himself to another cigarette. He dropped the match into the ash tray. 'Aye. He knows. But I don't. We haven't even begun to sort it out. That's why—after the coroner's verdict yesterday—we sent for you and why I'm so glad to see you here. You've got a reputation, Chief Inspector . . .' He looked round. '. . . and all of you. I hope you'll live up to it.' For a moment Masters thought Hook was growing moist about the eyes, but he went on talking. 'You see, Sally Bowker used to call me Uncle Fred. I'm not strictly her uncle. Her mother's only a distant relation of my wife's. But I've already explained what I felt about her. And I want whoever did it put behind bars for the rest of their natural.'

Masters got to his feet after the little silence that followed this statement. 'We'll do our best, sir. But I take it you have no suspect in mind? No lead you'd like to pass on?'

'Sorry. None. I just can't help you. Everybody liked Sally.'

'As far as you knew.'

'As far as I knew. And as I said, we couldn't begin to think of it as murder until yesterday afternoon, so we've done nothing at all.' Hook heaved himself to his feet resignedly.

'If I could have Miss Bowker's keys?' Masters asked.

'You can with pleasure. And what little paper-work there is. But won't you want to clock in at the Bristol?'

'Yes. But after that I'd like a look around. There's no need for you to bother, sir. Your desk sergeant can give Brant a street guide or directions. We'll manage.'

'Prefer to work alone, eh? Well, I don't blame you. But call in and see me. I want to be kept abreast of progress.'

Masters promised to keep Hook informed of developments, and they left him alone to sweat it out.

'To the pub?' Brant asked.

'Not yet. I want to look at the flat.'

'The locals will have been over it with a flea comb,' Green said. 'Can't we use their notes?'

'Hook just said they'd done nothing. All I've got is a post-mortem report and very little else. And in any case, can *you* visualize the layout of a building second hand?'

'No. But I don't have to. There wasn't a break-in, was there? She wasn't physically assaulted? There'll be nothing missing.'

'Somebody tampered with the contents of a bottle of insulin. How do you suggest they managed it?'

Green's jaw dropped slightly. 'You mean you think somebody did go in? Somebody with a key that fitted?'

'I'm keeping an open mind.'

'I'm pleased to hear it. Locked flats! Bottles that have been tampered with without being opened! I reckon our chances of pulling this off are flimsier than a stripper's knickers. I do, straight.'

Masters didn't reply. Brant had manoeuvred them slowly through a shopping centre and turned right along a road that curved past the railway station and then skirted a park. People were sitting and lying on the well-kept grass. Toddlers crawled and played beside their prams. Young-

16

sters, fresh out of school, were swarming over the swings and roundabouts of the playground enclave. Flowers blazed vividly and old men dozed on benches. The car turned left along the Bristol road and then, having diverged from the railway embankment, left again into a modern compound, built haphazardly of rows of maisonettes and blocks of flats, with doors of varying colours and pocket handkerchief lawns. Brant pulled up outside a small block—Wye House—standing like an old-time castle keep inside an outer bastion of up-and-over white-doored garages. Masters got out. There was no greenery just here. No natural beauty. The sun beat down on reflecting concrete. A few geraniums in an unwatered window-box were wilting. He felt the shallow steps to the front door hot through his shoe soles. The contrast in the foyer was so great he had to pause a moment for his eyes to become accustomed to the dim light. An indicator board told him that flat number five was upstairs. He led the way.

Sally Bowker's little home was on the left at the back of the block. Just four rooms. A living-room with a tiny kitchen off, a bedroom, and a bathroom-cum-lavatory. As far as Masters could see, on each floor were four of these little flatlets, all L-shaped, to form a box round the central stairwell and landings. Sally's front door gave on to an L-shaped corridor, on the inside of a similarly shaped arrangement of rooms. Directly opposite the front door were bathroom and kitchen, which together formed the shorter leg of the L. The doors to the living-room and bedroom were in the other leg. At the end of the passage outside the bathroom was an airing cupboard containing the hot-water tank. At the end of the other leg, outside the bedroom, was another, slightly larger, general utility cupboard. The bedroom window was on the end of the block. The windows of the other three rooms faced the rear.

When all four men were inside, the tiny hallway was

overfull. 'I don't know what I'm looking for, if anything,' Masters said.

'I'd have thought they'd have had somebody on duty here,' Green said wonderingly.

'I'd have expected it. But evidently they thought there was no need. And it's just as well from our point of view. Now. First of all the living-room.'

They followed him in. The furniture was contemporary and functional. The only signs of Sally's business interests were near the window. Here, on a red formica-topped kitchen table, was an artist's drawing-board with a wheel at the side for adjusting the tilt. Pinned to it was a plan of a window space with various items marked in. A long T-square lay across it. An anglepoise lamp, swung away; a vase with a posy of pencils a shapeless putty rubber; a sharpener like a small green dustbin; a straight edge with a metal ribbon on one side; a french-curve template; a compass and a craft knife. In the waste basket a heap of torn-up card. The pictures on the walls were bright marketing scenes. Masters touched nothing until he saw that the kitchen table had a drawer. He opened it. Photographs of window decorations. He went through them. He was impressed. He thought the *Show Off* girls certainly had the flair that Hook had claimed for them. In many of these pictures there seemed to be the recurrent theme of what the items displayed would do for the purchaser. Hook had said that in the Baby Shop they showed the effect of having a baby about the house. With electricity they showed the effect of power in the kitchen. Husband half-way through erecting shelves with the help of a power drill. Wife preparing a minute steak on an infra-red grill. Young daughter beating a cake with an electric mixer. Washer looking after itself. And so on. It looked authentic. There were empty food cartons lying about. Sawdust on the floor. Even splashes of paint on the folding steps. Masters realized the

18

appeal. It came from down-to-earth reality. It didn't stress the value of the various items. It stressed what each item would do to make life easier.

'You concentrate on this room,' Masters told Hill. 'Brant can take the kitchen.' He and Green went through to the bedroom. The bedclothes had been straightened. On the little table was a small aluminium case: a box less than six inches long, three wide, and an inch deep. Masters opened the snap lid gingerly. Inside was a white plastic lining divided into three longitudinal compartments. The near one was empty, but the nesting ridges suggested that it was intended to take two small bottles, on their sides, bottoms to middle. The central channel contained a metal cylinder, the full length of the box. Masters eased it out with a finger nail, and undid the screw cap. Inside was a syringe. He lifted the barrel. A fine needle was still attached. He could smell spirit. 'A carrying case,' he said. 'I suppose it keeps the needle sterilized. Smell.' He handed it to Green.

'Surgical spirit? No. I'm wrong. It's industrial.' He pushed the barrel back into the cylinder. 'By crikey, it holds the syringe tight. I s'pose that's to prevent breakage in a handbag.'

'That's a point. I wonder if she always carried it with her?'

'You mean somebody might have had a chance—while she was out, somewhere—of filling the syringe with something other than insulin?'

'If she kept it charged. It'd be easy, wouldn't it? Say it was in her handbag. She put it down and took her eyes off it. How long would it take? A couple of minutes?'

'This means we've got to trace her movements pretty carefully. When was she last seen alive?' Green asked.

'Damn! That's what I intended to ask Hook and I forgot. The old boy got me so involved with his emotional approach it completely slipped my mind. There's a phone in the living-room. Could you give him a buzz?'

Green went off. Masters glanced at the third compartment of the metal box. This was divided into two. In one half a pad of cotton wool; in the other a small, capped bottle of urine-testing strips and a spare needle. He turned the box upside down so that the contents slid gently out on to the table. He examined the lining. It was slightly buckled and just a little discoloured along the tops of the ridges. For a moment he wondered why, and came to the conclusion that it represented nothing more than fair wear and tear on a piece of comparatively fragile equipment that was used frequently and came into contact regularly with industrial spirit and insulin. He took the cap from the bottle of reagent strips. He tipped them on to his hand, and noted the dark brown colour of the impregnated part of each matchstick. He put them back carefully, making sure that the little desiccant pack went in, too. He closed the lid of the box.

He looked round the rest of the room briefly. Saw nothing to interest him and went to the bathroom. After opening the door he stopped. A momentary, evocative sourness in the air met him. Then it was gone. Imprisoned in the hot room, it had escaped through the newly opened door. For a moment he couldn't place it. Then it was recalled by his own reactions. He felt slightly nauseated. That was it! Vomit. Somebody had recently been sick in the bathroom. He called Hill.

'Smell?' Hill answered. 'I can't smell anything. A bit stale, perhaps, through being shut up, but all houses and rooms get like that.'

'I think she was sick,' Masters said. 'See what you can find.'

Masters left Hill and met Green in the hall. Green wrinkled his puggy nose. 'What's that stink?'

Green would never know how Masters blessed him for that remark. 'You smelt it?'

'Just a whiff. As though a little pocket of it passed me. What was it?'

'Vomit, I think.'

'Then for Pete's sake, light up that pipe of yours.'

'What did Hook say?'

'He wasn't there. The Station Sergeant says she was last seen, he thinks, by Brian Dent about ten twenty on Saturday night.'

'He thinks?'

'He's sure, but he didn't have the facts in front of him.'

'Thanks.'

'What if he brought her home and came in with her?' Green asked. 'It's a Chubb lock. He'd only have to pull it to behind him as he went and there'd be no sign of his having been here.'

'Having done what?'

'Changed the insulin. She could have left him alone long enough for all sorts of reasons. While she went for a whizz or changed her clothes, or anything.'

'He was closest to her. We'll bear him well in mind.'

Hill joined them, saying, 'I would say she must have missed the pan when she puked. Just a bit. Probably one splash went on the floor. There's a rag there—on the U bend—which I think she used for wiping up. Probably didn't rinse it very well afterwards. Feeling too ill at the time, I expect. Anyhow, it's all dried out now and smells a bit sour.'

'Could forensic do anything with it, d'you think?' asked Masters.

Hill grimaced. 'Maybe. I'll bung it off to them if you like. But I'm not all that hopeful because it has definitely been rinsed. It's not as if there'd be a lot of work on.'

'In that case, hang on to it. If we find we need to know what she ate on Saturday we ought to be able to find out locally. If not, we'll send the rag off.'

Brant joined them. 'There's not a sign of anything unusual in there, Chief. Nothing to do with diabetes or medicines. Not even an aspirin.'

'Thank you. In that case, we'll go and clock in at the Bristol.'

2 |

After they were installed at the Bristol, Masters felt unable to settle. It was six o'clock. Time to have a bath and a drink before dinner. The unwinding part of the day when most people like to take their ease and enjoy themselves. This evening, with a golden sun tumbling westwards and lengthening shadows, when the world outwardly seemed a good place, he felt he wanted to be up and doing. He sat in his room, smoking reflectively. He supposed the most miraculous organ of murder was playing with all stops out in the case of Sally Bowker. Right on his particular wavelength. Had she been sick? He thought he'd nosed it out. If she had, had it any bearing? To him it seemed it might well be significant. He wished to hell he knew more about the girl's disorder. Were diabetics more prone to other illnesses than other folk? Did their bodies react more violently to stimuli that in other people would be shrugged off with little or no discomfort? Green had been right. Here, from the outset, he himself was uneasy. No bliss in ignorance for him. He had to know. With a grimace he heaved himself up out of the armchair. There was one person who could tell him. Hook had said that Dr Sisson was up to date on diabetic treatment. Masters picked up the phone.

Dr Neville Sisson was in the middle of evening surgery. His receptionist was doubtful whether he would wish to be disturbed. Masters said, 'Please tell the doctor that I insisted you should interrupt him. You know who I am?'

'I'm afraid I don't. You've said you're a Chief Inspector Masters . . .'

'From Scotland Yard.' Masters was just faintly surprised and disappointed that his name carried neither recognition nor weight. 'I'm here to investigate the death of Miss Bowker.'

'Oh! That's different. I'm sure Dr Sisson will talk to you about *her*.' Masters thought he detected a note of pique in the receptionist's tone. Immediately he wondered whether the receptionist was jealous of the attention the doctor had paid to an attractive girl. Of the concern he had shown for her. It was a subconscious suspicion. Without a pause he said, 'In that case, would you please put me through to him.'

'Sisson.' The voice was deep. The type of immature deepness that reminded Masters of a boy whose voice has just broken and not yet completely settled down. He guessed it was a cultivated deepness, adopted to impress.

'Detective Chief Inspector Masters of Scotland Yard. I should like to meet you, doctor.'

'When?'

'This evening if possible.'

'Well, I'm free—I hope—after I've eaten. By about nine o'clock.'

'Can I see you then?'

'You can. But I'm on call, so there's no guarantee of an uninterrupted chat.'

'I'll risk that.'

'As you like. D'you know where I live?'

'If it's at the surgery I have the address.'

'Fine. I'll expect you. Now, if you'll excuse me, I've got a dozen patients waiting.'

'Thank you. Sorry to have interrupted you.'

Masters felt the conversation had been far from satisfactory. Sisson had raised no objections to an interview, but he hadn't been completely enthusiastic. There had been just a hint of unwillingness in his attitude. And when he got impressions of that sort during a murder inquiry it made Masters want to think. He chose the bath as the best place in which to ruminate. It wasn't a really comfortable pallet.

It was too small for his great size. When he lay back his knees were bent up, out of the water. But he stayed there for a quarter of an hour, apparently doing little more than gazing at the wall opposite. In fact, at one moment he found himself counting the courses of tiles.

When they were having dinner he told Green of his conversation with Sisson and the coming interview. 'I'd like to come with you,' Green said. 'I want to learn something about diabetes.'

'Right. We'll walk. Leave here about ten to nine.'

The sergeants were discussing Double Gloucester cheese. Wondering how it got its name. They agreed on the possibility of double strength but not as to how it was arrived at. Hill said when he got back to London he'd ring the Milk Marketing Board at Thames Ditton for an explanation, because to his mind, double strength or not, the cheese was mild. Masters, unusually for him, took no part in the gastronomic discussion. He'd been paying little attention to what he ate, and still seemed preoccupied with his own thoughts. 'We're up the creek, aren't we?' asked Green.

'I wouldn't say that. Not just yet.'

'Hook couldn't suggest a suspect. How does he expect us to?'

'Fresh minds. Emotionally uninvolved. Onlookers seeing more of the game. That sort of thing.'

Green tried to wiggle a strand of meat from between two teeth with his tongue. 'It doesn't often work like that in our game. The locals who know the background are more in the picture. Where do *we* go for honey? Hook says emphatically that the lad she's engaged to didn't do it. What other contacts have we?'

'Her partners?'

'You really think two other little artist lasses would know enough about diabetes to pull this off? Or that they'd ruin what sounds like a thriving business by doing in one of the leading lights?'

'If you don't like them there's the doctor. According to Hook he's knowledgeable enough.'

Green grimaced. 'We'll see, won't we?'

'And his receptionist. I told you I got the idea that she wasn't one of Sally Bowker's greatest admirers.'

'That sounds more like it. When a nice bit o' stuff gets murdered it's usually by some rival. But we'd have to find out what or who she was rivalling.'

Masters got to his feet. 'I know. It could be somebody who thought she had a better right to Brian Dent's affections. Or somebody who thought her boy friend was too taken up with Sally for the situation to be bearable. We can't tell. But we will.'

'I'm pleased you're so confident. Are we going now?'

They walked from the hotel to the centre crossroads with its one corner oddly embattlemented. By now there were few cars and even fewer people on foot. They could walk abreast down Eastgate to the corner of the side street with an arrow indicating the public library and museum. About here the buildings were of stone, pale grey and crumbling in places. Most of the older dwelling houses were now offices, devoid of any of the external touches—gardens, flowers, curtains—which must at one time have made them attractive homes.

It took them several minutes to find their way from here. Narrow streets, backing the main shops; smaller alleys leading off. A serpentine way, past a public lavatory and a makeshift car park. At last they came to it. A double-fronted house with wooden bays painted a dingy green. Four steps up to the door. The small area in front paved over, with grass and weeds growing in the cracks. A cube biscuit tin in the porch with a stick-on label: 'Please place urine-specimen bottles in tin'. A bronze plaque with white lettering: 'Dr N. B. Sisson M.B. B.Ch. Physician and Surgeon'. The original surgery times had been changed. Little stuck-on squares of newer bronze gave the alterations. Under the bell it said: 'Please Ring'. Masters, after a glance at his watch, did so.

Neville Sisson was a big man. Nowhere near as big as Masters, but a useful scrum-size. He appeared to be loosely built, slumping into his pelvis, which gave him heavy haunches and a sloppy appearance. His black hair had been crew-cut half an inch long all over, and his side whiskers came down to his ear lobes. His eyes, like his skin, were brown, and his teeth stood out brilliant white. His tie was little more than a thin rag under a crumpled collar, and as he stood at the door he tucked the ends in behind the button of his jacket. His trousers hung low on his hips and wrinkled above fawn shoes that needed polish. Masters said, 'I've brought Inspector Green with me. Do you mind?'

'Not in the least. Come in.'

There was a waiting-room notice to the right, and a surgery notice to the left. Sisson ignored them and led the way up stairs covered in linoleum. Their feet tapped out a rhythm as they went up. The first floor landing, square and spacious, was carpeted in drab haircord. Through half-open doors Masters could see a bathroom and kitchen. Sisson headed for a door leading into the front room on the right of the house.

Here there was more comfort than had appeared elsewhere. Four armchairs, all different, but comfortable looking. A coffee-table radiogram. Bookcases and drinks cabinet. An old-fashioned white marble fireplace with a stone jar of yellow Spanish iris on the hearth. An electric clock and two silver candlesticks on the mantelpiece. Two small oils in gilt frames, almost obliterated but apparently views of Edinburgh Castle from widely separated points on Princes Street. Two others in black frames—obviously old—of little girls in long frilly frocks and wide-brimmed hats standing in daisy fields. The carpet was a handsome, self-figured green: the curtains a browny-fawn velvet that went well with it. Scattered about were newspapers and journals, giving the room a lived-in appearance.

'Where would you like to sit?' Sisson asked.

They chose their seats. Masters inquired: 'Are you a married man, doctor?'

'Not me. Haven't had time to think about it yet.'

'Not even to think about it?'

'Well . . . you know how it is.'

Masters took out his pipe and asked permission to smoke it. Sisson got up and poured three whiskies. When they were all settled again, Masters said, 'I know nothing about diabetes and comas. Chief Superintendent Hook told me you are an expert. Could you enlighten me as simply as possible?'

Sisson balanced his glass on his chair arm. 'It's not a disease, you know,' he said.

'What is it, then?' asked Green.

'You could call it a disorder. But strictly it's what's known as a metabolic defect.'

'Could you explain that?' Masters requested.

'You don't know what metabolism means?'

Green said, 'He will. I don't.'

'It's the physical and chemical processes within the body by which food is converted into living substance.'

'You mean it turns boiled beef and carrots into living flesh?' Green asked.

'Not quite. It organizes food into a state where it can be reconverted into simpler compounds like starch and sugar, which in turn change to fat or release energy for the use of the body. That's a very simple and not wholly accurate

28

picture, but it will do.'

'Got it,' Green said.

'Good. Now, to complete the metabolism, sugar needs insulin to oxidize it for use as energy in the muscles. O.K. so far?'

Masters nodded.

'If the body can't produce enough insulin of its own to use up all the sugar, you get spare sugar being discarded by the body—in the urine. Hence the name of the defect—diabetes mellitus, which means honeyed urine.'

'How does this defect occur?' Masters wanted to know.

'Like any other defect, such as poor eyesight. You can be born with it, have it caused by accident, or as you get older you can gradually come to it.'

'But Sally Bowker was only about twenty-two . . .' Green said.

'I know. That's one of the tragedies. Kids as young as eleven can develop it—and up to about the age of thirty their type of defect is still known as juvenile diabetes, which is, incidentally, the worst form, because of all the demands made upon the body by young, active life.'

'How does it start?' Masters asked.

'By developing a defect in the pancreas. Or to give it the butchers' name, the sweetbread.'

'Seriously? You mean we eat . . .' Green said.

Sisson nodded. 'Now you know where it gets its name.'

'I'll never touch it again.' Green looked at Masters as though the latter doubted him. 'I won't, I promise you.'

Sisson went on: 'The pancreas has lots of little glands which produce insulin. Now, if those glands aren't working, or if only some of them are, we have to inject insulin to make up the body's requirements. Fortunately, most diabetics are not of this type. Most are what is known as maturity-onset patients. This means that in later life, together with most other parts of the body, the insulin glands are beginning to get a bit tired, and so don't do their stuff properly. If that's all that's happened, we very often don't have to inject insulin. In lots of cases we can give pills that ginger up the glands to make them start working a bit harder. That produces enough insulin for older people, because they are less active and so have smaller appetites. But when we can't ginger up the tired glands, then we have to resort to insulin again.'

Masters said, 'Let me see if I've got this right. A girl like Sally Bowker, still in the flush of youth, hasn't lived long enough for her glands to begin to wear out. They've just packed it in for some reason or another, and so there's no alternative to injected insulin. Correct?'

'Absolutely. All young diabetics have to be given insulin.'

Masters relit his pipe. As he put the match in the tray he said, 'Many thanks. That's cleared that up. But I'm puzzled about diabetic comas. Shouldn't she have taken a sugar lump or something?'

Sisson stretched his legs and rested the heel of one shoe on the other toe. 'Let's put it this way—just for simplicity's sake. There are two types of coma a diabetic can fall into. One's what we'll call a sugar-coma, meaning they need sugar; and one we'll call an insulin-coma, meaning they need insulin. Those aren't the correct names, but they'll make it easier for you if you'll remember that the substance mentioned in the name is the substance they are short of. Better still, call them sugar-hunger and insulin-hunger, then we shan't get confused. Are you with me?'

'I'm on your heels, doc,' Green replied. 'If I keep this up I'll be applying for medical school next.'

'The more the merrier. But to get back to the Chief Inspector's remark about the sugar lump. Most people regard sugar as poison for diabetics. It isn't. It's the staff of life. They should all carry it with them to suck at any time, because it's true that by far the most common type of coma is sugar-hunger. And the coma can come on fast. But it goes even faster if you can get some sugar into them. They'll literally recover in the middle of being given a glucose drink. They should be able to dose themselves as soon as they start to perspire and feel woozled. Most of them do. But insulin-hunger is a different—and far more serious—thing. Fortunately it's not nearly so common. And the answer is to inject insulin. But because it's a more serious condition, diabetics who suffer from it at any time usually need medical attention and nursing.'

'How quickly does it come on, and go?' Masters asked.

'Much more slowly than sugar-hunger, both coming and going. It takes anything up to forty-eight hours each way, unless . . .'

'Unless what?'

'Unless there's something to aggravate it and bring it on much more quickly.'

'Meaning?'

'When diabetics get other illnesses, like 'flu or a bilious attack, etcetera, they need more insulin to combat them. Not less, as some think. You see, they believe that because an illness means they lose their appetites, they don't need insulin. This is wrong. In fact they need more to help them fight the ailment. And if they omit to take the insulin—or don't increase it if necessary—they start to suffer from insulin-hunger, and the symptoms of a coma start coming on.'

'What symptoms?'

'Thirst. Desire to urinate. Tiredness. Drowsiness. Nausea. Probably abdominal pain. Shortness of breath.'

'Are they the people whose breath starts smelling of

peardrops?'

'That's it.'

'How does that come about?'

'Well, with no insulin to oxidize the sugar, the body starts to utilize the fat for energy. It burns it up, but there's not complete combustion. Just like when you make a coal fire you produce warmth—which is your object—but you also produce smoke, soot and ash. The body gets rid of some of this through the urine—the ash, as it were—while the soot remains as a sort of poison to make them ill, and the smoke comes out as acetate on the breath. These people lose weight very rapidly.'

'I can see they would if they burn up their fat. Now, Miss Bowker. She died in a diabetic coma, brought on by insulin-hunger?'

'Yes.'

'Because she injected herself with useless insulin?'

'That is my belief.'

'Even though these comas are slow to start?'

'That's the only thing that puzzles me. Why she didn't get help while she was still capable of doing so.'

'Even though she was sick? She vomited, you know.'

'She would. That's one of the symptoms. It's caused by the accumulated poisons of excessive fat metabolism. They urinate a lot and they vomit. This dehydrates them. The body loses all its fluid. As much as ten or fifteen pints. With the fluid go the basic minerals. As a result, their circulation collapses, their pulse becomes feeble and god knows what else. They look like Belsen inmates and they are in immediate danger of death. Insulin alone won't save them then. They've got to have the fluid they've lost put back straight away. And even when that's done they can die from shock and heart failure. If there's nobody to help them . . .' He didn't complete his sentence. The thought of Sally Bowker, ill and helpless, seemed to affect him more than Masters expected a doctor to be affected by the death of a patient. Without regarding doctors as in any way callous—any more than he was himself—he was of the opinion that they encountered death so often it inevitably began to have less effect on them as time went by—again, just like himself.

'When did you last see her—before her death?' he asked.

'On Saturday morning. I like to reserve that surgery for permanent patients. Patients who have to come and see me at intervals for long periods or, as in the case of diabetics, for the rest of their lives.'

'You examined her?'

'Thoroughly. They bring charts of their urine tests, you know. I looked at Sally's record pretty carefully, and tested the sample she brought. I do that. Just to make sure they're not backsliding or making mistakes with their own tests. And I gave her an overhaul. Examined her feet pretty carefully . . .'

'Why her feet?'

'Because the extremities are a diabetic's most vulnerable spot. Any cut or abrasion on the feet is liable to go wrong. I'll not go into the medical reasons, but take my word for it, gangrene can set in very easily because their feet are poor healers.'

'Are you in a position—ethically—to tell us the result of your examination?' Masters asked.

Sisson turned towards him. He said gruffly, 'To hell with ethics in this case. Sally Bowker was one hundred per cent fit. Not a snuffle in her nose or chest. Not a flutter of her heart. One hundred per cent fit. That's why, when she died in a coma shortly afterwards, I was suspicious. Insulin comas take time to come on—maybe up to forty-eight hours—as I've told you. If she'd been starting one that would render her helpless by Saturday night, I'd have spotted some of the symptoms twelve hours before.'

'You're sure?'

Sisson glowered. 'Of course I'm sure.'

'Please don't misunderstand me. I'm not doubting the thoroughness and skill of your examination. I'm wanting to establish without doubt that a coma which could knock a girl out by midnight would be showing some signs during the morning before. The first signs couldn't have appeared, say, in the middle of the afternoon?'

'Not a chance.'

'Alternatively, could the coma have come on later than Saturday night?'

'It could. But I'll take my oath it didn't.'

'What makes you so sure?'

'Lots of reasons. First of all, the body takes a long time to die, and Sally had been dead at least twenty-four hours when I saw her on Monday evening. That means she'd died no later than Sunday evening. A coma such as this doesn't kill even the old and decrepit in a flash. If she became comatose by midnight on Saturday, it means that she was lying there less than twenty hours. A girl as fit and well as Sally would take at least that time to die.'

'That sounds convincing.'

'But there's something else which makes me sure this coma came on fast. Sally was a very sensible, practical girl. She knew what the symptoms of coma were and how to combat them.'

'Had you taught her?'

'Thoroughly. She knew that at the first signs she was to take more insulin. This she had done. The dose taken from the bottle shows that.'

'Does it? How?'

Sisson accepted a cigarette from Green and sat back thinking for a moment. Masters watched him carefully. At last the doctor said, 'Let's go through my reasons from the beginning. Sally was on long-acting insulin. That means she only had to inject twice a day.'

'At twelve-hour intervals?'

'Not necessarily. Actually the times of injections are governed by the times of main meals. To get ready to counteract the food that the body is about to get, you need to inject about half an hour before the meal. So I'd given Sally a programme which meant an injection half an hour before breakfast and half an hour before supper.'

'She ate breakfast?' asked Green. 'Not just a glass of orange juice?'

'She ate hearty.'

'Was she allowed to?'

Sisson grinned. 'These juvenile diabetics are put on a diet like everybody else. But because they're so active they need more food, so as long as they don't go too far over the score, they're not restricted nearly as much as most people think. Certainly the first rule for diabetics is "Never go hungry".'

'I see. The little weighing-scales are completely out of fashion.'

'Gone years ago. You can adjust insulin intake these days fairly easily to make up for minor indiscretions. It's a good thing to take great care, of course, but the thought that they're not in an absolute strait-jacket helps them mentally.'

'I can understand that. But now to get back to Sally Bowker . . .'

'Oh, yes. When she came to me on Saturday she'd already had her morning injection, and she told me she'd got just enough left for her before-supper dose. That was how it should be. I prescribed just enough to carry her through to the day of our next appointment.'

'Isn't that a bit risky?'

'Not at all. She could always call at any time if the need

35

arose. But I like to give them just what they need each time. Then they can get a nice, fresh supply for the next four weeks.'

Masters tapped out his pipe on the palm of one hand and dropped the ash into the tray. 'So you gave her a new prescription which we know she took to the chemist that morning. At seven in the evening—or just before supper time—she'd have taken the last dose of the old stock. The new should have been started at breakfast time on Sunday. Right?'

'Quite right. But I'm positive that having died on Sunday evening, she could not possibly have been in a fit state to inject herself on Sunday morning. I'm positive that the latest time she would have been able to do this would have been midnight Saturday.'

'I'll accept that for the moment. Now can you explain why she didn't get help.'

Sisson leaned forward. 'I'm certain she was taken by surprise. She must have suddenly become aware that the coma was on her. She acted quite properly in giving herself another dose of insulin. Thinking that would work she probably didn't call anybody and then, by the time she realized the injection wasn't going to reverse the symptoms, she was probably too ill to phone. State of collapse, I'd have thought. Flaked out on the bed and never came round.'

'Then how do you account for her going to the lavatory to vomit, and clearing up afterwards?'

'That was probably the first symptom. And you know yourself that if you have a good clear-out, you feel better, if only momentarily. At least until the next wave comes. You probably feel so much better you can pull the chain, clean your teeth ... all sorts of things. Then you're sick again. And so on. Until, as I see it in Sally's case, you lie down virtually exhausted, waiting for recovery. Instead you

36

become comatose.'

Masters got to his feet. 'Thank you, doctor. If nothing else you've given us a basis for working on.'

Sisson stood up and said, in a rather embarrassed tone, 'I'm glad. I want to help.'

'Because she was your patient?'

'Yes.' It was a snapped answer. Slightly too brusque.

'Nothing more?'

'How d'you mean?'

'She was an extremely personable young woman.'

Sisson reddened under his tan. 'You're not suggesting . . .'

'I'm suggesting nothing. But I thought you did.'

Sisson stared at him for a moment, and then said: 'O.K. You might as well know. I thought she was everything a girl should be.' Then he changed his tone. 'But that doesn't mean I ever . . .'

'Of course not. I realize you would respect her too much ever to give her a hint of your feelings. But just off the record, had you hopes?'

Sisson toed the carpet, uncomfortably. 'You're a nosey bastard, but yes, I suppose I had. After she'd been diagnosed as diabetic. I thought that there might be just a chance . . .'

'Of Dent throwing her over?'

'Not really. Brian wouldn't dream of it. But he's a bit under his parents' thumb, and his mother's a protecting old hen who wouldn't want her boy tied up to an invalid. She was heard to use those very words. So I thought perhaps Brian might yield to pressure. And if he had!'

Masters smiled. 'I know.'

Sisson said, a bit shamefacedly, 'Well, I could have given her expert care.'

'And more, I've no doubt. Thank you very much indeed. I expect we shall meet again. In fact, can I come running if I find something I don't understand?'

Sisson held out his hand. 'It'll be a pleasure. I'll confess I wasn't very keen on meeting you tonight. I thought you'd just ask a lot of tomfool questions I couldn't answer—like the local lot. God, how they floundered! But you arrived and asked for information and advice. Your attitude was a revelation to me, I can tell you.'

'That's the way we work, doctor,' Green said. 'I've been telling Chief Inspector Masters all day that we were going to be up the creek unless we got our bearings about diabetes. So our very first job was to look up the expert and consult him.'

Sisson grinned at Masters. Neither said anything. Green shook hands and the doctor showed them out.

By now it was dark. A warm, soft darkness that felt pleasant after the heat of the day. Masters started to stroll slowly. 'Come on. Step lively,' Green said. 'We've only got about ten minutes before the bar closes.'

'We're resident.'

'Maybe we are, but they won't send draught Worthington up to rooms. Only bottles.'

Masters increased his pace. They reached the hotel in silence.

They took the first drink quickly so as to get a refill before time was called. 'Did you get all that the doc gabbled about?' Green asked Masters.

'I think so. Didn't you?'

'Oh I got it. I expect I could almost repeat it word for word.'

'I expect you could.' Green's memory was phenomenally good.

'But I'm just a bit puzzled by it.'

'Sleep on it. It'll sort itself out.'

'Maybe. But it's given us some leads hasn't it?'

'Such as?'

'Why wasn't she missed before Monday evening?'

'That's a good point. And tomorrow, being Saturday, we should be able to find out.'

'You've got a plan?'

'I'd like you to take on her two partners. I propose to see Dent. If you want Brant with you, take him. But if not, he and Hill can go over the block of flats where she lived . . .'

'Wye House?'

'That's right. We might pick up a few reports from somebody who saw or heard her on Saturday night.'

'I'll go alone.'

'Right. Brant can take you in the car before he starts on Wye House.'

'That's the lot?'

'Not by any means. I want a word with Sisson's receptionist and Dent's parents. And I've no doubt a few others might occur to us before we're through.'

Green picked up his beer and drank deeply. He said, inconsequentially, 'I wonder if diabetics are allowed to drink beer? If not, in spite of doctors saying they can lead normal lives, they're missing one of God's better inventions.'

Masters put his empty tankard down. 'We can discuss that tomorrow, too. I'm for bed now.'

'Me, too.'

At breakfast time the next morning Green asked for sausage, bacon, eggs, tomatoes and sauté potatoes. 'Don't stint yourself,' Hill said. 'Have a few kidneys as well.'

Green, who had appeared in a pale grey Palm Beach suit said, 'I'm never going to eat offal again. I've been hearing things I don't like.'

'I've never seen that suit before,' Brant said. 'Where've you been keeping it?'

'The government paid for it. Remember when I was sent out to Cyprus? Had to have something to wear in all that sunshine in the Med. This is it. I was fitted three times for it.'

Masters was reading the *Telegraph* as he ate. Green didn't enlighten the others that it was Masters who had suggested to the A.C. that the suit should be paid for out of public funds, had helped Green choose the material and had bullied his own tailor into doing a rush job for his subordinate. Green could never have done this for himself, but would never acknowledge the fact. Masters appeared to be paying no attention now. He was dressed in light grey himself—a check bookie suit, cut hacking-style and built to suit his huge figure. He smiled inwardly at what appeared to him a naive conversation: astute enough to realize that Green was slightly embarrassed at wearing this particular suit, because it was different in colour, weight and cut from his usual reach-me-downs, but ideal for the present heatwave. He also realized that in his oblique way, by stating he had not paid for it himself, Green was acknowledging the help he had been given.

When his plate was set before him, Green rubbed his hands in anticipation before beginning to eat. Masters lowered his paper, poured himself another cup of coffee, and said, 'Seeing you enjoy yourself over that little lot reminds me of something you said last night.'

'Wha'?' Green said, with his mouth full.

'About beer. Can diabetics take beer? We don't know much about what they can and can't eat. I was thinking about it before I went to sleep.'

'I might have known you'd have some beer in your bonnet.' Green laughed at his own joke. Getting no response from the others, he went on: 'Everybody knows diabetics have to be bloody careful about what they eat and how much.'

'Do they? Sisson last night said a diabetic should never go hungry. Probably they're not allowed to tuck in, like you, to their hearts' content, but exactly what can they eat?'

'No sticking in till they stick out, but if they can never see green cheese but their een reels, then they're allowed to have a bit. That what you mean?'

'Something of the sort.'

'How will it help us if we know?'

'Just an idea I had.'

'In other words you're not talking.'

'I can't explain unformed theories.'

Green sneered, 'Theories!' and got on with his breakfast.

'We went for a jaunt round the town last night,' Hill said.

'And?'

'We stopped and looked in a chemist's window. They've got a series of little books on every disease there is. Things like bronchitis, arthritis, migraine and so on. For people who suffer from them to buy so they can understand what their complaint is all about and to cope with it. There's a diabetic book among them. If it's for use by the patients themselves it's bound to have instructions on diet, I'd have thought.'

'Excellent,' Masters said. He looked at his watch. 'I don't know what time the shops open here, but it must be any minute now. Buzz off and get me a copy. And while you're at it, have a word with the pharmacist. He might have other leaflets he can let you have.'

Hill put his napkin on the table and got to his feet. 'Can you give me half an hour?'

'Until ten if you like.'

Green wiped his mouth with an air of satisfaction. 'D'you want me to wait?' he asked.

'No. That's why I told Hill he could have until ten o'clock. Brant can drive you to Cheltenham while I'm waiting. If you're too long in getting there they may be out for the day before you arrive.'

'Going to see the other two girls?' Brant asked. 'Now I know why he's got his snazzy suit on.'

Green lit a Kensitas and flicked the match at the sergeant. 'Come on, Po-face, wheel out that old crate of yours while I have another drink of tea. I'll expect you at the front door in five minutes.'

Masters was smoking his first pipe of the day at the door of the Bristol when Hill returned, carrying a small handful of booklets. 'I've got quite a bit here,' he said. 'The chemist gets all sorts of reprints of papers sent to him. The manufacturers use them to advertise their goods—diabetic tests and foods and what-have-you.'

'Lovely. We've got a bit of time before Brant gets back. I want the two of you to question the occupants of Wye House, but you can drop me at the doctor's surgery on the way. Until we go, we'll comb these booklets. I want to find information about diabetic diets in young adults.'

They turned through the foyer of the hotel and out of a

door at the back. Here the garden was provided with green-painted iron tables and slatted, folding chairs. The dew had gone, but the sun was not yet high enough to be unpleasantly warm. Hill, however, took his jacket off before getting down to work. Masters put his feet up and started looking through the first of the pamphlets.

They read for some minutes in silence. Then Hill said, 'There's an advert here for beer.'

'Diabetic beer?'

'No. Carlsberg. It says, "A more than fair exchange. Don't deny yourself a glass of Carlsberg, but do remember that it has to be used by exchange as the carbohydrate content is not negligible." What does "by exchange" mean?'

'That's one of the points I've picked up. Every food or drink that has carbohydrate in it is given a value that is taken off the total the patient is allowed for the day. Does it say how many grams of carbohydrate there are in Carlsberg?'

'Ninety four calories, six point seven grams of carbohydrate in half a pint of Export Lager.'

'There you are, then. A hundred grams of carbohydrate according to this book is 1,000 calories. Though it doesn't seem to work out like that with your beer.'

'Perhaps it averages out at that, Chief.'

Masters looked at a chart in his book for a moment. 'Maybe it does. Fifteen ounces of cauliflower and two ounces of orange both have five grams of carbohydrate.' He turned the pages again. 'Ah. Here we are. "The different foodstuffs vary weight for weight in the calories they produce, and a doctor, when planning a diet, should take caloric needs for heat and energy into consideration as well as carbohydrates and proteins." That sounds clear enough. So we know they can substitute half a pint of Carlsberg Export for three ounces of orange or a pound and a half of cauliflower. Interesting.'

'Here's a dietitian saying they can eat near normal diets.'

Masters grunted. He was in the middle of an article about young diabetics on insulin. The diet for these people was said to be much more liberal ... no need to measure caloric intake as long as carbohydrates were balanced by injections ... take plenty of proteins and reasonable amounts of fat ... remember soft drinks, beers and sweet wines contain sugar which must be counted when working out the diet ... fortunately, dry wines and spirits contain negligible amounts of sugar and may be taken in moderate quantities by the young diabetic who does not need to watch calories ... and so on.

Masters began to feel he was getting the hang of it. A youngster like Sally Bowker could eat a diet adequate to fulfil her appetite and energy requirements just as long as she took sufficient insulin to counteract it. He put down the pamphlet and relit his pipe. He was still sitting there thinking when Brant found them. Masters said, 'I'll keep these. I'll read a bit more later. Would you mind going up to my room and putting them on the dressing-table?'

Hill did as he was asked. He rejoined the others as they were getting in the car. Masters directed them to Sisson's house.

'Will the doc have finished his surgery by now?' Hill asked.

'Possibly. But it doesn't matter if he hasn't. I want a word with his receptionist.'

Masters found the surgery door locked. Obviously patients had to arrive before ten. After that the door was locked and the last visitors were allowed out, one at a time, and the door relocked behind them. Masters pressed the bell. There was no response, so he pressed again. Still no answer. He was about to ring a third time when an elderly

44

man let himself out. Masters stopped him from pulling the door shut behind him.

'You'll not be allowed in there.'

'You think not?'

'I know not. She'll be after you.'

'She?'

'That young woman. Reg'lar spitfire she is. Treats you like a criminal. If the doctor wasn't so good he wouldn't have no patients. She'd drive them all away, she would. Stands at the door with a stop watch in her hand waiting to bolt up, she does. It's a job of work for her. Nowt else.'

'Thanks for the warning. I'll take my chance.'

'Well, you looks big enough to take care of yourself.'

The old man went slowly down the steps. Masters stepped into the hall. As he did so a woman dressed in a near imitation of a nurse's uniform came out of the second door on the right of the passage. 'You're too late to see the doctor,' she snapped. 'Pull the door to behind you as you go.'

To her surprise Masters continued towards her. 'You heard what I said?'

'I could hardly fail to. But I chose to ignore it.'

'Surgery ends at ten.'

'I've no quarrel with that.' He stood towering over her. 'In fact, that's why I came at this time. So as not to interrupt Dr Sisson in the middle of his business.'

'Who are you?'

'Not a patient. Detective Chief Inspector Masters. I believe you and I have spoken on the phone, Miss . . .?'

'Oh, the policeman.' She was sharp featured with pale, gingery hair, showing wispy under her cap. Her eyes were yellow, under faint ginger brows. The eyelashes were almost non-existent, and her fact was pale with a sprinkling of freckles. Her body, fairly thin, was nevertheless well proportioned under the spotless, well-ironed uniform. Her legs and feet were neat, and she stood proudly, like a turkey cock at dawn, nothing abashed by his presence and size. There was the same sneer in her voice that he had detected over the phone. 'The doctor has still got three patients to see.'

'Never mind. I'll wait.'

'And then he has his domiciliary visits.'

'No doubt. I'll still wait.'

'In that case the waiting-room door is behind you.'

'Not in there. I'd like to speak to you, Miss . . .?'

'Don't keep calling me Miss. My name is Nurse Ward.'

'Very good, Nurse Ward. Can we use your room? I see it has Receptionist written on the door, so I presume it is your room.'

'I have nothing to say to you.'

'It really would be a pity to spend a nice afternoon in a stuffy police station when ten minutes now would suffice.'

'Are you threatening me?'

'Yes.'

The affirmative took some of the wind out of her sails. Simply because she hadn't expected it. For a moment she stared at Masters. Then: 'Policemen can get into trouble for using threats.'

'Can they for threatening to ask you to accompany them to a police station? Think again, Nurse Ward. And stop being obstructive or I'll begin to think things about you you won't like.'

'More threats?'

'Certainly. People who put difficulties in my way during a murder inquiry find life made difficult for them in their turn. I'm a mean man, Nurse Ward. A mean man.'

As he knew she would, she turned and led the way into her room. Here the doctor's metal filing-cabinets lined one wall. A yellow varnished desk with a staggered row of prescriptions for collection occupied the centre of the room. In one corner was a white wash-hand-basin with a pedal bin below it. A row of shelves held pharmaceutical samples, and a small table an electric kettle and cups. She sat on the chair at the desk. He took the other one.

'Now, Nurse Ward, let's discuss Sally Bowker.'

'Her medical facts are professional secrets.'

'But not her movements, her personality, her gaiety and so forth. She was an extremely popular girl, I understand.'

'With the men, perhaps.' She sounded prim: something more than disapproving.

'Not with her own sex?'

'Hardly. When she couldn't leave the men alone.'

He paused a moment to consider this. There was a decided amount of nastiness here. He switched his line.

'You're not married, Nurse Ward?'

'You can see I'm not. But I can't see what that has to do with Sally Bowker.'

He said blandly, 'Can't you really? Now you're a trained nurse . . . you are, aren't you?'

'S.R.N.' It was said proudly, with a toss of the head.

'Exactly. Well, your training has been not only professional, but vocational, too. That means you're interested in people and, no doul you've learned a good deal of psychology in your time. Am I right?'

'If you mean I can see as far through a brick wall as the next person, you're right.'

'Good. Now, you're an exact replica of Sally Bowker in many ways . . .'

She set her face. 'I don't see how you make that out.'

'You're a young, attractive, unmarried woman, earning your own living. Miss Bowker was the same, I believe?'

The flattery seemed to soften her, 'Attractive, but not

much character.'

'I see. You've just made my point. I would expect a girl like you, like Miss Bowker in many respects, but with professional training to back up your female intuition, to be able to give me a better insight into this girl's character than any man. Men, I suppose, were attracted by ... what? Her prettiness?'

'That's it exactly. And her disgustingly forward manner.'

'You mean she deliberately made a play for other men although she was engaged to be married?'

'That's exactly what I mean.'

'I'd like to know about it. You see, now you've told me she was a fast young lady, it opens up all sorts of possibilities. It may mean that some man . . .'

'You're not suggesting Dr Sisson . . .'

'Dr Sisson what?'

'Was in any way responsible for her death.'

'No. Certainly not. Should I?'

'Of course not.'

'Nurse Ward, are you worried about Dr Sisson?'

'No.'

'But Sally Bowker did make a pass at him?'

She nodded. 'Every time she came.'

'And last Saturday morning?'

'Worse than ever.'

'Would you tell me how you know? Were you present?'

'I'm always on hand when the doctor examines women. It is part of my duty.'

'You go into the surgery with them?'

'Not into the surgery. The surgery is directly opposite the waiting-room. Directly opposite here is the examination room. It communicates with the surgery. The door between the two rooms is kept open. It is my job to be in the examination room whenever a female patient is in the surgery. Then, of course, if the examination room is used, I'm on hand.'

'Do I take it that this procedure is as much in the interest of the doctor as the patient?'

'It is for his protection.'

'In case some woman accused him falsely of unprofessional conduct?'

'Yes.'

'Is it usual practice for the nurse receptionist always to be within hearing-distance?'

'Dr Sisson is a young, unmarried man.'

'So you made this arrangement personally—without direct orders from Dr Sisson?'

'His orders are that I should be present when any woman patient is examined. How am I to know which will be examined and which won't unless I'm always there?'

'I see your point.' Masters was inclined to think that this very strict interpretation of her duties was more to enable Nurse Ward to keep her eye on the doctor than for the doctor's protection. She was keen on him herself. He was sure of that. 'Sally Bowker made some flippant remarks to him last Saturday?'

'Flippant? She arrived here in a mini-skirt that was positively indecent. In bare legs and sandals. She flounced into the doctor, lifted her skirt so that he could see everything she'd got on—what little there was of it—and asked him to look at some lumps she'd got on the tops of her thighs.'

'Lumps?'

'They were nothing. Lots of diabetics get them. On the injection sites if they use one spot too often.'

'Why use one spot?'

'Because the skin and tissue gets hard and numb and so it's less painful to inject on the same spot. But when they

49

do it too often they raise lumps.'

'Permanent ones?'

'They go away if left alone. She knew that. She just used it as an excuse for . . . for displaying herself. There's plenty of room on anybody's thighs for injections, but if you're the type that won't wear anything but a mini-skirt, showing all you've got, you've got to inject very high up all the time. The lumps she showed Dr Sisson were almost . . . well, all I can say is that the underclothes a respectable woman would wear would have covered them completely.'

Masters nodded. In his mind's eye he could see young, attractive Sally Bowker, with her long, languid legs holding up the side of her skirt to show the edge of a little bikini pantie. The sort of picture that intrigued him vicariously; that would set the pulse of the young doctor—in love with her—racing; and would anger this nurse—so little older in years than Sally Bowker, but decades older in prudery—in love, in her turn, with the doctor, and jealous that he should be granted, in so guileless a fashion, this intimate view of another woman's charms. He felt he had now got Nurse Ward so worked up, so indignant, that she would continue to talk if he led her carefully.

'What happened? Did the doctor advise her what to do?'

'Dr Sisson was very correct.'

'And that was the only incident?'

'Not by any means. She asked him about having children.'

'You mean that as a diabetic girl, about to be married, she wanted to know whether it would be safe to have a family?'

'Yes.'

'Is there anything wrong in that?'

'What she actually said was, "Brian says the first thing he wants to do after we're married is give me a baby. Shall I let him or are you going to suggest the Pill?"'

'What was Dr Sisson's reaction?'

'He told her what every diabetic woman knows.'

'Which is?'

'That though there may be an hereditary factor in diabetes, it is unlikely that it will emerge in the children when only one partner to the marriage is diabetic, particularly if there is no history of diabetes in either family.'

'You know all about it.'

'I should. I'm trained. I have worked in a diabetic clinic.'

'Of course. With Dr Sisson?'

She nodded.

'You left hospital service specifically to become his receptionist?'

'He advertised. I applied. He knew my work and chose me out of quite a large number of applicants.' There was pride in the voice. But he knew she'd got it all wrong. When opening a new practice, Sisson had wanted efficiency to get the business off the ground. Nurse Ward was fooling herself into thinking that he had chosen her for her personal attraction. There would be no point in enlightening her.

'After the doctor had given his advice on having children, what next?'

'He renewed her prescription for insulin and told her to make an appointment with me for four weeks time. As she was leaving the surgery she said to the doctor, "Brian will be thrilled to know he can give me babies. He's a keen businessman you know, and his one fear has been that he wouldn't have a son to carry on." Disgusting.'

'Forthright and very modern, perhaps. But was it so bad? After all, a doctor's consulting-room is a sort of confessional. A place where patients bare their souls and minds as well as their bodies.'

'Not to the point where they try to ... to seduce the doctor.'

'You felt that was what she was trying to do?'

'Of course she was. Showing herself off and all that talk about being given a baby. Why couldn't she say having a baby?' She looked at Masters under lowered eyelids. 'There's a nine-month difference between the two. Being given a baby is a sexual act and nothing to do with the doctor. Having a baby is giving birth and *that* is his concern. Not the other.'

Masters got to his feet. 'Thank you for telling me all this. It helps, you know, to realize just what sort of a person the victim was. By the way, did you see her again after she made the appointment?'

It seemed to Masters that Nurse Ward hesitated a moment before she answered, 'No.' It was an unequivocal answer, with none of the supporting words of explanation that he would have expected from the average person.

'Can I see the doctor now?' he asked.

'Wait here. I'll see.'

She went out, smoothing her unruffled dress as she went. He could imagine her halting in the passage to finger the stray strands of hair into place before knocking on the doctor's door. She was back almost immediately. 'Dr Sisson will see you in a few moments. He has nearly finished with the last patient.'

She filled the electric kettle and plugged it in. From a wall cupboard she took sugar, milk and instant coffee. 'Is Dr Sisson engaged to be married?' Masters asked.

She slopped the milk. The question had caught her off balance.

'No. He isn't.'

'I have always understood that it is desirable for a doctor in general practice to be married. The patients like it. But I suppose a lot of women would find the life of a doctor's wife these days very wearing . . .?' It was a question. He wanted her to react. She did.

'Not if they understand the problems.'

'Could they? Before experiencing them, I mean?'

She turned and faced him. 'A nurse would. The correct wife for a doctor is a nurse. To help him, understand him and his work . . .' She didn't finish. She turned back to the coffee making, as though aware she might have said too much.

'That's what I thought,' Masters said.

A moment or two later he was being shown into the surgery by Nurse Ward, who was carrying a small tray with two cups of greyish-looking coffee on it. Sisson was in his shirt sleeves, and although the window was open there was a faint smell of ether in the air. Sisson said, 'I've about ten minutes in which to drink this, then I must be on my way.'

Nurse Ward left, closing the door behind her. 'I want a bottle of insulin,' Masters stated. 'Can you give me a prescription for it?'

Sisson gulped at the hot coffee. Grimaced because he'd burnt his mouth, and put the cup down. 'Quite honestly I don't know the form in cases like this,' he said. 'Strictly speaking I can't prescribe except for genuine need. Where police demands fit into the picture I just can't say. As far as I know there's nothing laid down to cover these circumstances.'

Masters, sipping his coffee, said, 'I don't want to snarl up the works. Would a pharmacist sell me a bottle?'

'Unlikely. Although I don't know. Insulin isn't a scheduled drug. It's just one of those items a chemist doesn't expect to sell over the counter, and so he wouldn't provide it except against a prescription.'

'Perhaps just a note from you would do the trick. I'd pay cash.'

Sisson nodded. When Masters left a few minutes later he had the doctor's signed explanation and request to supply one 10 ml phial of Rapitard insulin for police purposes. He knew that he hadn't really needed the note, but he felt he'd had to have some excuse for calling on Sisson's receptionist.

Green was enjoying himself in Cheltenham. He had the knowledge that he was unusually and topically well-dressed, which, left wing though his views were, nevertheless made him feel good. The journey had been through pretty countryside looking at its best. The day was beautiful. Cheltenham Promenade looked attractive, with its excellent shops and its gaily dressed shoppers. And on top of all that, a chat with two personable girls in prospect.

Their flat, in an Edwardian house some way behind the College, was on the top floor. Green climbed the first flight laboriously, and found the front door of the second-floor flat alongside and at right angles to that of the first-floor apartment. It had an illuminated bell. He pressed it and somewhere above his head heard a two-tone chime. There was the sound of light feet skipping downstairs, and the door opened. Green said who he was. 'I'm Clara Breese,' the girl said. 'Come in, won't you?'

They were on a small landing. The colours were so startling—purple and yellow—and the travel-poster murals so garish that for the moment Green forgot to look at Clara Breese. By the time he'd recovered his wits she was leading him up an internal flight of stairs. Then he looked. She was in a short, pale pink quilted housecoat and mules to match. As she went ahead of him he had an excellent view of a fine pair of bare, firm legs and thighs. He watched the tendons tauten and the muscles move as she stepped upward. They turned at right angles. Two steps more and they were on a little square landing off which all the doors appeared to open. Except for a small window on the bend of the stairs the only natural light on the landing was borrowed through a stained-glass panel through the clear bits of which he could see the kitchen.

'Hang on a sec,' Clara Breese said.

As Green stopped a voice from a room on the right called, 'Who is it, Clara?'

Clara poked her head round the door. 'Get up, lazy-bones. It's the law. Scotland Yard.'

'Oh, hell. At this hour?'

Clara Breese turned to Green. She was dark and handsome. Almost black hair parted in the middle, with very little hint of wave in it. A well-shaped, sun-tanned forehead, fine black brows, a straight nose and eyes as merry and black as a West Highland terrier's. Her neck was smooth, with no hint of line or wrinkle. Her hands were, Green thought, on the big side, but looked extremely well cared for with the nicest shaped nails he'd ever seen. The housecoat was too full and couthy to show her figure, but he noted that it stood proudly enough at the breast to promise well. 'Come into the sitting-room,' she said. 'We haven't done our weekly housework yet, but at least there's a chair to sit on.'

He followed her in. A big, L-shaped room, with a flat window and a wooden wainscot a yard high all the way round. This was grey. The walls were in sprigged yellow paper. Above the picture rail, where the walls curved gracefully inwards to the flat of the ceiling, was a band of lavender colour, fading into white around the central chandelier.

The furniture was hotch potch. Unmistakably the collection of two different personalities. The two armchairs were inundated with glossy magazines. Clara cleared one heap for Green. He noted two he had never heard of or seen before—*Graphis* and *L'Oeil*. He wondered about

55

them. He could recognize *L'Oeil* as French. Was it full of nude studies? Or as innocuous as the *Homes and Gardens* that accompanied it? He sat down and asked if he could smoke. 'Yes, do,' Clara said, and then went to the door to call, 'Win! Heat up the coffee and bring it in, will you?' She waited for the muffled reply and then came back to clear the other chair for herself. 'You must excuse us. We hadn't an inkling you were coming and Saturday is our Sunday, you know.'

'Why's that?'

As she sat she tried unsuccessfully to close the gap at the bottom front of the housecoat. 'Nobody will let us near a shop to window dress on Saturdays. They're much too busy. But on Sundays we get a free run because the shops are shut. So we're always up and doing on Sundays. It's the busiest day of the week with us.'

Green thought for a moment. 'What about last Sunday? Weren't you worried when Sally Bowker didn't turn up?'

'Not in the least. In fact we didn't know she didn't turn up. Win and I were busy in Cheltenham. Sal had an appointment in Gloucester. We didn't begin to get worried till Monday tea-time. The shop she was supposed to have done on Sunday had been trying to get us all Monday. But we were out until four. Then they tried again and got us. One of their people had been waiting for hours on Sunday to let Sal in. They wanted to know what we thought we were playing at.'

'Then what?'

'I tried to get Sal on the phone. I thought she might be under the weather—being diabetic, poor old thing. But I got no reply. Then I rang the shop where she ought to have been working on Monday. When they, too, said she hadn't shown up I began to get worried. Win and I went over to Gloucester, saw Brian Dent, and he contacted the police.

They got hold of the master key and found her.'

'Master key? Where from? There isn't a caretaker in Wye House?'

'No. It was in the agents' office.'

'Who are the agents?'

'Haven't a clue.'

Winifred Bracegirdle came in with a coffee tray. Having been given more warning of Green's presence, she had taken the trouble to dress properly. She was short and well built. She had dark hair and a naturally dark skin. An elfin face, almost triangular, that needed dark lipstick to show off the pleasant mouth and excellent teeth. She was a mature woman in miniature. A nice bosom, Green thought, and excellent legs. She had to wear very high heels to give her any height at all. She smiled at him. 'Good morning. How d'you like your brew? Black, white or khaki?'

She poured and handed round the coffee and squatted on a pouffe. 'Hold the fort, Win,' Clara said. 'I'll take mine with me and get dressed and in my right mind.'

'I should think so. You must be embarrassing this poor man, sitting opposite him in your dishabilles. Have you got any pants on?'

'Linings only,' Clara grinned, and as she went through the door, added, 'Transparent nylon ones.'

Win smiled above her coffee cup. She doesn't care, you know.'

'What about?'

'Anything.'

'What's anything?' Green said patiently.

'Oh, whether she's wearing pants or not. Whether she lives in complete chaos. Whether she shocks people. Whether she loses things, boy friends—anything.'

'Boy friends? She sticks to numbers?'

'Now she does. Although . . .'

'Although what?'

'Oh, just that she didn't always.'

Green sensed that Win was not being quite as forth-coming as she might be, or had intended to be. 'So she had a steady at one time?' he asked.

Win nodded.

'Who?'

'Oh, just some chap.'

Green hazarded a guess. 'Brian Dent, perhaps.'

'You knew.'

'No. But you were being so cagey it was easy to see you were trying to hide something. You wouldn't try to hide the name of somebody not important to me. So speak up. She went steady with Dent at one time?'

Win nodded. 'For about six months.'

'Then what?'

'He teamed up with Sal. After that Clara didn't seem to care very much. A different one every night.'

'Fair enough. She can play it any way she likes. But you hinted just now that with Sally Bowker dead . . .'

'I didn't mean anything. It's just that the way seemed open again—for Clara and Brian, I mean.'

Green lit another Kensitas. 'When did you last see Sally Bowker?'

'Last Friday afternoon. I'd done her some stickers and she came to collect them.'

'What did you do on Saturday?'

'I cleaned up the flat and did some shopping in the morning. Went swimming in the afternoon. And had a date at night.'

'And Miss Breese?'

'I think she went to Gloucester after lunch. I didn't see her till Sunday morning.'

Green asked for the name and address of Win's date. While he was writing it down, Clara came in, wearing a pale-blue summer frock and white sandals. Green noted

58

her toe nails were painted cherry-red and, unusually for him, approved. 'Miss Breese,' he said. 'When did you last see Miss Bowker?'

'Here, last Friday.'

'Not on Saturday?'

'No.'

'Did you go to Gloucester on that day?'

Clara looked across at Win. 'You've been gassing as usual, Win.' She turned back to Green. 'Yes, I went there. But not to see Sally.'

'Would you care to tell mé what you did do?'

'I went to visit an aunt.'

'How long did you stay with her?'

'I didn't see her. She was out when I called.'

'So what did you do, Miss Breese?'

'I had tea in a shop. Went round the cathedral. Then went to the cinema, and came home by the ten o'clock bus.'

Green made notes of the places Clara said she'd visited. He closed his book and asked, 'Were all three of you good friends?'

'Very,' Win said.

'As far as I know,' Clara said.

'Yet Miss Bowker left you?'

'Only to deal with our Gloucester business,' Win explained. 'It had nothing to do with . . .'

'With what, Miss Bracegirdle?'

'You might as well know,' Clara answered him. 'Brian Dent and I were friendly at one time. Then he fell for Sally. I expect Win's already told you.' She sounded disillusioned.

'I didn't. I swear I didn't. He guessed. Didn't you?'

Green nodded. 'Even detectives can't guess like that without some hint to tell them they're getting warm,' Clara said.

'Don't fall out about it. I had to know, some way or another,' Green comforted her.

'Why?' Clara asked.

'Somebody killed her. We want to find out who it was.'

'Is that all? Or have you some more questions?'

'Just one. Has either of you ever been a nurse?'

Clara looked across at Win and smiled sweetly. 'Didn't you do a bit of studying, ducky, before Sal and I asked you to join us? When you thought you'd never get any other job?'

Win reddened. 'Yes. I did. What about it?'

Green got to his feet. 'Thank you, ladies. Could you tell me where I can catch the bus for Gloucester?'

At Wye House, Hill and Brant were calling on those occupants who were at home. There were eleven other bachelor flats, besides Sally Bowker's, in the block. Their questions were restricted mainly to asking when each occupant had last seen the murdered girl. The two sergeants expected little joy, and that is exactly what they got. But it was very noticeable that every person they talked to—young and old of both sexes—spoke very highly of Sally. In the most enthusiastic terms. And not simply because she was dead. Her neighbours gave the definite impression that as far as she was concerned, beauty really did live with kindness.

By midday they had managed to see all but one of the tenants. The last one, a Miss Wombrugh, had been away all morning. The others were certain she had merely gone shopping and would be back for lunch. 'Shall we forget her?' Brant suggested. 'She'll not have anything more to tell us than the rest. And that's nothing.'

'I'd say go home now,' Hill said, 'but for the fact that she lives next door to Sally Bowker. She might just have heard or seen something last Saturday night.'

Hill was right. Miss Wombrugh was a well-set-up woman of fifty. The sergeants, without knowing who she was, saw her walking smartly, despite a heavy basket, up to the front door of Wye House. The two, standing on the step, watched her approach, and stood aside as she drew near. 'What a beautiful day,' she said. 'You look a little lost. Can I help you?'

'If you are Miss Wombrugh, madam . . . ?' Hill asked.

'I am she.'

'We are police officers. We've been waiting in the hope of seeing you.'

'Have you? I'm so sorry. In this hot sun! And I took an unconscionable time over my coffee in the *Bon Marché* this morning. Had I not done so I should have been home much earlier. I do apologize.'

'No harm done, ma'am,' Hill said. 'Let me take your basket.'

She handed it over as though it happened every day of the week. She had a dignity and an obvious ability to accept courtesies of this sort as a natural thing. She led the way upstairs. Her upright figure, good legs and sensible dress for the weather would have put many younger women to shame. She opened her flat door and they found themselves in an exact replica of the one Sally Bowker had lived in except that this one was at the other back corner of Wye House, and so was a mirror image.

She invited them to sit, and without asking poured them all sherry, saying, 'I have no other drinks in the house.' There was no further explanation.

She sat down. 'Well, gentlemen, what do you wish to ask me? I assume it is in connection with the death of my late neighbour.'

Hill said, 'We're from Scotland Yard, ma'am. There's a team of us down here to investigate Miss Bowker's death. There are several lines of inquiry going on. One of them is to ask the occupants of Wye House if they saw Miss Bowker, or heard her, last Saturday evening.'

'I have told the local Chief Superintendent that I saw Sally with her fiancé about twenty past ten last Saturday night.'

'Where, ma'am?'

'On our little landing outside, and on the approach road.'

'If you could expand that a little, ma'am.'

'Of course. I'm falling into the same trap that I often warn my girls at school about. I teach English to the upper forms. I keep reminding them that though they may be familiar with the subject they are writing about, they must assume the reader is not and that explanations must be full and logical.'

'Quite,' Hill said.

'I was walking home last Saturday night from a supper engagement with a colleague. It was a pleasant evening, and I felt no need for a cab. I left at ten or a few minutes after, knowing it would take me almost exactly a quarter of an hour to get here. Shortly after I left the main road—where the sign says "Private to residents only", Mr Dent passed me—or rather, overtook me—in his car. He had Sally with him. I know the car, of course, and I could see the occupants quite easily because the road is well lit and the hood was down. It's a coupé—an E-type Jaguar I believe it is called—with a very distinctive look. Only a minute or so later I reached the front door. The car was drawn up there. I came upstairs, and there were Sally and Mr Dent at the door of her flat.'

'Doing what? Saying good night?' Brant asked.

'That is what I imagine they were doing. But not in the traditional style.' She smiled. 'No long, lingering kiss as in the novelettes. Sally was actually just inside her hallway. The door was half open. Her right hand was about shoulder height on the jamb, and though I couldn't see her left hand, from the position of her arm I should say she was holding the door-knob inside. She was facing her fiancé who was just outside in the passage. I got the impression that she was about to go in, and that he was about to go away. And I think the scrap of conversation I overheard supports my belief.'

'What did they say?'

'I am sure I heard Sally say, 'I know it's quite early, but I've a big day tomorrow and I feel a bit *m'yer*.'

'A bit what?'

Miss Wombrugh smiled. 'It's a modern expression—both facial and vocal. It is compounded of a grimace and an onomatopoeic sound supposedly resembling that associated with the rather unpleasant act of vomiting.'

'*M'yer?*'

'Quite right.'

'This is quite important,' Hill said. 'Miss Bowker definitely said she felt *m'yer?*'

'Without any doubt at all. Knowing Sally to be a diabetic, I felt just a twinge of worry, but as I stopped by them to open my door she smiled quite gaily and said good night to me. Mr Dent said good evening, too. And before I was fairly indoors I heard him say good night to Sally, too. I think the kiss came at that point, but it must have been a short one, because before I had finished hanging my light coat in the landing cupboard, I heard him going downstairs and his car starting. As I said it was a pleasant night, the windows were all open, and there is no mistaking the noise that particular car makes when it starts up.'

'And that's all?' Hill asked. 'You didn't see or hear her again?'

'Certainly I didn't see her. But after I'd made my nightcap and had it, I went to the bathroom to prepare for bed.

63

Now, if you are familiar with these flats, you will know that my bathroom neighbours Sally's.'

Hill nodded.

'And you can probably guess, today's building standards being what they are, that the dividing wall is made of a single thickness of breeze blocks, laid on their edges. What my father—who really was a master builder—would call "rat-trap" fashion.'

Hill nodded again.

'Bearing that in mind, I think—but I can't be sure because I was cleaning my teeth at the time and what I heard may have been the rumblebelly plumbing—I think I heard Sally retching.'

'What did you do?'

'I stopped my scrubbing, turned off the tap and stood listening with my mouth full of toothpaste foam which began to dribble down my chin. I heard no sound at all, so I presumed I had been mistaken. Otherwise I should have gone to her.'

'You didn't think of going just in case?'

'I'm ashamed to say I didn't. You see, were Sally to have been all right, and in bed—as she had suggested she would be half an hour before—and possibly asleep, I should have been categorized as a nosey old cat for waking her up. And I shrank from that, partly because I like to live at peace with my neighbours and to keep my nose out of their affairs and partly because it is not easy to say to any young woman, "I thought I heard you making a noise in your bathroom." As it is a lavatory also, and noises, even when clearly heard through party walls, may be deceptive, the greatest exception may be taken. To say the same thing to a diabetic girl may suggest that you are taking an interest in her condition so great as to constitute an invasion of her privacy.'

'We appreciate your difficulty,' Brant said.

'I'm afraid, also, that I consoled my conscience with the thought that if she were really in trouble and needed my help she could quite easily come to me. I know now I must have been wrong, for she never came, and yet she died.'

'In a coma.'

Miss Wombrugh shook her head. 'She was a very nice child. I liked her very much. She had the trick of being able to treat me as an equal. Usually, these days, the young manage to make the middle aged feel so inferior, as though the added years were some form of leprosy.'

'She was a popular girl?'

'I think you will find that those who knew her will miss her gaiety and prettiness as well as her kindness. I know I shall.'

The sergeants got to their feet and took their leave. 'One o'clock,' Brant said. 'Time for a dirty great pint—iced.'

4

Green reached the Bristol at about the same time as the sergeants were first meeting Miss Wombrugh. He looked about for any of the other three, and finally found Masters sitting at the same little table in the garden as he had used earlier that morning. Masters was again reading the pamphlets Hill had brought him.

Green said by way of greeting, 'Anything in those?'

Masters looked up. 'A host of facts. Incidentally you'll be pleased to hear that insulin-dependent diabetics can drink beer.'

'The real stuff?'

'Real and genuine. And while we're talking about it, how about seeing if you can see a waiter?'

'I've been working, while you've been sitting here on your fat backside . . .'

'No, no. Besides, you're on your feet. Mine's a long, cool pint of draught Worthington, by the way.'

Green stomped off to get a waiter or the beer. Masters gathered his papers together to make room on the table. When Green came back with two foaming flagons he drew out a seat for him.

Masters took a long draught and then asked, 'How's Cheltenham?'

Green gave him a full account of the conversation he had had with Clara and Win. When he'd finished, Masters said, 'Quite a few points there.'

Green nodded and drained his glass.

'Clara Breese?'

'Could be. Everything fits. Jealousy at losing Brian Dent. And that rather woolly sort of jaunt in here last Saturday. But I'll tell you what. She's worth ten of the other girl in my opinion.'

'Maybe. But a good woman will fight hard to get her man.'

'A woman scorned?'

'That, possibly. Anyhow the lads will have to check her story. See if anybody remembers her at the tea room, cathedral, cinema, last bus and so on. Even then it might not be enough. There's a possibility she could have gone to all those places, just as she said, and still have had time to visit Sally Bowker.'

Green nodded glumly. Masters went for more beer. When he got back, he said, 'And are you thinking what I'm thinking about that master key?'

'You mean do Dent and Blackett hold it?'

'Hook said they were the biggest property agents in town.'

'That's what I thought. I'll check on Monday.'

'Why not now?'

'It's Saturday. Nearly one o'clock. They'll be closed.'

'Not they. Estate agents keep open all day Saturday. That's when they do most of their trade. Remember working men can't look round houses at any other time. Try 'em.'

Green stood up, took a pull at his beer and then went indoors to phone. He entered the booth in the foyer and looked up Dent and Blackett's number. When he was through, he said, 'My name's Bishop. I'm looking for a bachelor flat.'

'Oh, yes, Mr Bishop? Well I'm afraid it's not going to be too easy . . .'

'I suppose not, but I've just heard that there's a flatlet vacant in Wye House—where somebody died recently.'

The voice at the other end sounded shocked. 'Oh, but I'm afraid we can't consider that at the moment, it's still in the hands of the police . . .'

Green put the phone down and returned to Masters.

'It's theirs all right.'

'Thanks. That's another line we'll have to follow.'

'And how! If young Dent had free access to his girl's flat
...' He didn't finish the sentence. His beer claimed his
attention.

'And I'm interested in the news that those girls work on
Sundays. Whoever killed her probably counted on it. If so
it indicates that it was somebody who knew her movements
pretty well.'

'Like her boy friend? Could he be regretting it?'

'What?'

'The prospect of marriage to a diabetic?'

'It's a thought.'

After a pause, Green asked, 'What about you?'

Masters gave him an account of the talk with Nurse
Ward. When he'd finished, Green said, 'Another prime
suspect. Thought the doc was going overboard for her, did
she? Killed her to stop it. Could be. What about her saying
she didn't see the Bowker girl again after she left the surgery? You sounded as though you didn't believe her.'

'I didn't.'

'So there are three suspects so far. Dent, Clara Breese
and Nurse Ward. Could be worse, I suppose after only one
morning's work.'

The sergeants appeared at the back door of the hotel.
Green shouted across to them, 'You'll have to bring it out
yourselves from the bar. And while you're at it, make it
four.' He turned back again to Masters. 'You're pretty sure
this Nurse person did see Sally Bowker again on Saturday?'

'No. No. Not specifically.'

'And what does that mean?' The beer he had already
drunk was beginning to make Green sweat. He took his
jacket off and hung it on the back of his chair and mopped
his brow with a red and white spotted handkerchief.

'Either she did see her or she didn't.'

'It depends on how loosely we interpret the word "see". If I said to you, "Have you seen the estate agents yet?" you might reply, "Yes. They manage Wye House." You would be giving me a factual answer and the information I wanted. But you wouldn't be giving a strictly truthful answer, because you didn't "see" the agents, you phoned them.'

'I get it. So you think Ward phoned Bowker.'

'I should have said a phone call was unlikely. But I think she could have been discussing her with a third person. Go over it carefully—imagine it. Question: "Did you see Sally Bowker later?" Expected answer: "No. Not after I let her out of the surgery." That's the typical reply. Agreed?'

Green nodded.

Masters went on: 'But if somebody says, "No," and then pauses, you get the impression there's a bit more to come. And it would have come if what was about to be said had merely been confirmatory and explanatory. But it wouldn't come if it were not confirmatory: if the speaker suddenly had second thoughts: if she'd been about to say something like, "No, but I was talking about her to Lizzie Dunk that afternoon." See what I mean?'

'Yes.' Green didn't sound too sure.

'All I'm saying is that I got the impression that Nurse Ward was going to say more, and then thought better of it. And because I'm feeling suspicious, I'm trying to guess what she had intended to say.'

Green mopped his brow again. 'You're probably right. She probably discussed Bowker with the doctor.'

'Maybe, but that would be so likely and unremarkable that I don't think she would have deliberately avoided mentioning it.'

'She might—if the memory of it was painful. Say she had

spoken to Sisson, and because what she'd overheard had made her mad with jealousy, some of what she said wasn't too discreet. Sisson would tick her off, wouldn't he? And anybody who's been carpeted likes to forget it or keep it quiet.'

Brant and Hill approached carrying two tankards each. 'Sorry to be so long,' Brant said. 'They're thicker in that bar than protesters in Trafalgar Square.'

Masters took his beer from Hill, then turned to Green. 'What you said just now is quite logical and probably the right answer. But we'll bear other possibilities in mind.'

Hill drew up a chair and sat down. He drank deep and then asked, 'Fruitful morning?'

'Hard to tell yet,' Masters said. 'What about the occupants of Wye House?'

Hill made his report on the morning's work. When he'd finished Green commented, 'That knocks one of our suspects out. If Brian Dent didn't go into the flat it makes a porridge of our theory about him having a key.'

'Why?' Masters asked.

'Well, if he'd wanted to go in for any reason surely it'd have been commonsense to go in to say good night to his bird. A lot more natural and less likely to cause comment.'

'But the girl was feeling sick by the time he got her home,' Masters objected.

'Maybe she was. But he'd want to get inside to doctor her insulin. That's commonsen . . .' He stopped in mid-word and stared at Masters. 'By crikey! That carrying case! Her insulin was in a carrying case. She'd been toting it around in her bag and she'd been out with him!'

Masters smiled at Green's amazed tones. 'The penny's dropped?'

'This gets worse,' Green complained. 'The insulin could have been tampered with either in the flat or outside.

We're not getting any closer. We're getting further away from the answer.'

'Not us,' Masters said. 'We're simply getting more elbow room. Having alternatives is a jolly sight better than being stuck with just one rigid set of possibilities.'

Green didn't appear comforted by this philosophy. 'It's a set of Sunday undies to a G-string that she and young Dent went cavorting all over the county that day. And we'll have to follow them up.'

Masters finished his beer and got to his feet. 'I'm going to have a salad lunch, and then back on the job.'

'Doing what?'

'I think it's time you and I saw Dent. The boys can check up on the movements of Clara Breese last Saturday.'

Green put on his jacket. 'What about the Ward woman? Aren't her movements important?'

'They are. They can take her in, too. We'll give them the score while we eat.'

The offices of Dent and Blackett were situated in a street leading from the main road to the cathedral close. The waiter they asked for directions told them how to get there. 'Go past Woolworth's and turn right where you see an arrow on a lamp-post. You can't miss it because it's only a bit of an alley about a hundred yards long.'

The alley was just wide enough to take a car. The pavements on either side were about two feet wide. Far too narrow for Masters and Green to walk abreast. They passed antique shops and second-hand bookshops with dim interiors and apparently little trade. Going their way were several small parties of sightseers in holiday dress, with cameras and sunglasses. Intent on doing the cathedral, part of the fabric of which Masters could see just beyond the end of their tunnel-like street. So intent was he on seeing as much as he could of the building which loomed ahead that he almost missed what he had come out to find. 'Come on,' Green said. 'Mind your head.'

A brass plate on old black woodwork. A window, protected by an overhang, with photographs and details of property. A low doorway. Another dim interior. Masters stooped and entered. The floorboards were old, uneven, and over a foot wide, with a patina of age enhanced by *O Cedar* floor polish, the smell of which gave the place a homely, welcoming atmosphere. The clerk behind the desk asked if he could help.

'Mr Brian Dent, please.'

'I'm sorry. Mr Dent isn't here.'

'You mean he's out?'

'No. I mean he doesn't work on Saturdays.'

Green said. 'Why not, if the office is open?'

'Mr Dent has nothing to do with property sales. He is an architect. His studio and office are upstairs, but his business is entirely separate from ours. No five-day week for us, worse luck.'

'Is he likely to be at home?'

'That I can't say, but I don't think you'd better call on him. Monday morning would be better. I can make an appointment for you.'

'No, thank you.'

'I'm sure he wouldn't thank you for going to his house. He's just ... well, his fiancée died rather tragically a few days ago, and I think he'd far rather not be bothered just now by ordinary business.'

'It's extraordinary business we're on, brother,' Green said.

'Oh!'

'Police,' Masters explained. 'Would you please ring his home and tell him we're on our way to see him.'

The clerk picked up the phone as they started to leave

the office.

'Why tell him to do that?' Green asked. 'Dent'll be warned.'

'He must know we'll be getting round to him soon, and that chap in there would have phoned him in any case. He didn't say so, but he knew we were policemen. We can't disguise ourselves that easily.'

Masters turned towards the cathedral. Green, tagging along behind, said, 'That's not the right way to Dent's house.'

'It is unless you want to walk.'

'Taxi?'

'No. If the sergeants are doing their stuff they should be making inquiries here now, or soon should be. If we hang around a bit we'll see the car and they can give us a lift.'

As they left the alley, the full splendour of the cathedral opened before them. Green stopped in his tracks. 'I go to chapel,' he said.

'So? It doesn't hurt to look at a church.'

'That's what I mean. You can feel the power of that place at this distance, can't you?'

The precincts had disappeared, to make way for a car park. The surrounding houses, which Masters presumed must once have belonged exclusively to members of the Chapter, were now turned into commercial offices. The place was a right of way for everyday business, and besides sightseers, townsfolk hurried to and fro with shopping-baskets and prams and briefcases, oblivious of the source of sacred power which towered above them, a stone-coloured silhouette against a hot, blue, sky, like a Canaletto original backing a modern populated canvas by Lowry.

'Worth a look, isn't it?' Masters said.

'Yes. But does it pay?'

Masters was a little surprised by this remark. Then he saw the board which had occasioned it. The cost of daily

73

upkeep was there for all to see, in the hope that those who visited would contribute. He said, 'You yourself said it was a power house. Does Battersea pay?'

Green grunted. 'I can't see the car.'

'In that case we'll go inside for a few minutes and you can help preserve history by dropping sixpence in the box.'

In the cool interior, Masters knelt. When he got up, he found Green standing by a model of the cathedral. He had put his sixpence in the box. The windows had lit up and an organ-music record had started to play 'Holy Night'. Masters saw that Green was completely fascinated. Near him stood two little girls in summer dresses. All three listened intently. Masters went to the door to look for the car. It was drawing in as he stepped out into the sunlight.

Brant dropped them at Dent's house. It was a single-fronted modern villa, standing very much alone, but with great width of frontage because the separate garage, level with the building line, had been connected to the main house by a flat-roofed car port. The newness and brilliant whiteness of the paint, in this sunshine, gave an air, not of rural England, but of some sub-tropical play centre. It struck Green as much as Masters. 'Old Dent must have gone a bust on this,' Green said. 'I'll bet he's got a swimming pool and tennis court at the back.'

Masters sent Brant back to the cathedral to pick up Hill. 'An E-type coupé in the shed?' he said to Green.

'That's it. Pop uses the garage, son the dutch barn. I wonder where mum keeps her scooter?'

The door opened as they approached. The hall was wide and carpeted all over in plain red. Masters guessed it was Brian Dent waiting to welcome them.

'Mr Brian Dent?'

'That's me. And you're the two policemen the office rang up about?'

Masters introduced himself and Green. He liked the look of Dent. Tall and not too heavily built, he wore a washed-out blue shirt and grey slacks with a pair of well-polished brown leather shoes. His hair was dark brown and fine, falling over his brow on the right: a natural unruliness that Masters thought would have its own attraction for girls. His eyes were brown, and his beard area fairly dark. The bare neck and throat were tanned, and a hint of hair showed inside the V of the shirt.

'Come in,' he said. 'Mum and Dad are on the terrace, but it's cooler inside—especially if there's a lot of talking to be done.'

He showed them into a sitting-room at the front of the house. Masters didn't care for it. It was very new and modern, but it was also absolutely rectangular without a break or an alcove anywhere. Where, in Masters' opinion, there should have been a fireplace, was a glass-fronted cupboard, with green baize-covered shelves on which was laid out a hunt in full cry. Without inspecting them closely it was difficult to say, in the dimness of their prison, whether each of the little china pieces was as exquisite as it gave the impression of being. Seeing him gazing, Dent pressed a switch, and concealed lighting flooded the scene. It took on life. The liver, fawn and white hounds, each scarcely an inch long, the mounts, the habits, and the quarry—a small scrap of a fox, perfectly proportioned, about to go to earth—breathed life and colour. Green said, surprisingly, 'That'll be German.'

'That's right.'

'Saw one just like it over there in forty-five. I wanted to loot it, but somebody beat me to it.'

'You? Loot?' Masters asked.

Green coloured. 'Actually I didn't get anything. But I'd

have liked that. It was in a corner cupboard. Like that one over there.' Green pointed to a corner of the room.

'Won't you sit down?' Dent said.

It was modern furniture. Square. Not really big enough for Masters who preferred armchairs that accepted and enveloped him when he sat down: feather-cushioned wing chairs with overstuffed rolling arms and plenty of depth from back to front. A chair that had no head rest was no armchair to him. And this room wasn't homely. It had everything; but everything was in its place. There were no newspapers lying about, no books left open. He thought Sally Bowker must have felt strange in a house like this after living in farmhouses, overcrowded flats and untidy studios. There was only one piece of furniture that intrigued Masters. It was Green's corner cupboard: carved oak with leaded panes so old that they scarcely allowed a view of the contents, except where labels were close up to the inside of the glass. Masters could just read some of them: La Ina, Courvoisier, Anisette, D.O.M. He could think of no better use for so fine a piece than to make it serve as a wine cupboard. He imagined the elder Dent had bought it at one of the auctions he conducted. If so, it said much—in Masters' opinion—for his taste. So much less garish than the modern cocktail bar one might expect to find in a room such as this. Masters thought he would have liked the piece for himself; thought he could just make out—now his eyes were growing accustomed to the dim light—the outlines of other bottles, and tried to guess their contents by their shapes. He was pretty sure of Vat 69 and Gordons when Dent, noticing his interest, said, 'Would you like a drink? I'm sorry, I should have offered . . .'

'No, no. Thank you. Not at this time of day. I was just admiring the cupboard.'

'It is rather splendid, isn't it? We're going to have an internal light fixed some day.'

'To switch on when the door opens?' Green asked.

'That's right.'

'Right, gentlemen,' Masters said, 'shall we get down to business? You know why we're here, Mr Dent?'

Dent nodded. 'Sally.'

'We'd like to know everything that happened last Saturday. So far we have visited her doctor whom she saw in the morning. She left the surgery, I believe, at about half-past ten. What do you suppose she did then?'

'Went shopping. It was her usual Saturday-morning chore, and I know she went last Saturday because she took her prescription to the chemist and got a fresh supply of insulin and she also went on her usual spree looking for suitable foods.'

'Suitable?'

'Sally could eat most things, but all the same she took great care to make sure her diet wasn't overloaded with fats and other high caloric items. She took a lot of green vegetables and fairly high protein stuff, and she was pretty particular to get the best there was. She'd shop around for it.'

'I see. That would take her up to lunchtime, I suppose.'

'Certainly not later. She ate on time. It helps diabetics if they stick to a very strictly timed routine, you know. One thing I'd learned through being with Sally was that she'd never allow herself to get peckish, and she always carried a sweet or a few sugar lumps in case she did. I think you can safely say she'd have lunch at one.'

'At home? Or in a restaurant?'

'Definitely at home.'

'How can you be sure? Did she tell you?'

'No. But she fought shy of restaurants. There was no real reason why she should have done, but as I told you she was very particular about her ten-gram equivalents . . . you know what they are?'

Masters nodded. 'The diet sheets list all the amounts of the usual foods that give ten grams of carbohydrate. If I remember rightly seven ounces of water melon equal a third of an ounce of sugar and they both yield ten grams of carbohydrate. Is that it?'

'Yes. And in restaurant food—or so Sally said—you never knew what was being used. I mean it takes three-quarters of a pound of tomatoes to give ten grams, but if they make tomato soup with all sorts of thickeners and add sugar to it and so on, a diabetic hasn't a clue what equivalents he's being dished up. And Sally said puddings were particularly bad in this respect. So she never went to restaurants if she could help it.'

'Not with you when you were out together?' Green asked.

'Sometimes. To places where she could be sure of a salad and stewed fruit sweetened with saccharin.'

'That must have cut down your pleasures quite a lot,' Masters said.

Dent said simply, 'A bit. We used to go out to eat very often before Sal knew she was diabetic. But we'd learned to do without since. There's plenty to do besides eating out, you know.'

Masters produced his pipe and tobacco. As he rubbed a fill in the palm of his left hand he asked, 'What were you proposing to do after marriage, Mr Dent? Were you going to live on a diabetic diet? Or would your wife have expected to cook two separate dishes each day?'

Dent laughed. 'Nothing like that. Diabetics eat the same food as anybody else, but possibly less of it.'

'No, Mr Dent.'

Brian Dent looked at Masters for a moment, and smiled in a puzzled way. 'Take a very common lunch,' Masters said. 'Roast beef and Yorkshire. A diabetic won't tackle

78

Yorkshire pudding. Won't eat roast potatoes. Won't eat creamed potatoes because of the butter and milk in them. But he will eat boiled potatoes. Potatoes with no extraneous flavouring and easily measured into equivalents. Rather daunting isn't it? Boiled potatoes for ever for a man who likes them roast, mashed, chipped, sauté-ed, fried and so on. And no Yorkshire! And no stewed fruit sweetened with sugar. And so on. In an endless list. Hadn't you thought of all this, Mr Dent?'

'Of course I had. My mother has pointed it out often enough even if I hadn't thought of it for myself.'

'Your mother? And yet you were contemplating married life with equanimity?'

'Of course I was. Odd as it may seem, I adored Sally. Wanted her.'

'Before she was diabetic.'

'And after. Only more so. The thought of her having diabetes—her injections, tests and diets—only made me want her more.'

'Out of pity, perhaps.'

'Pity be damned. It was love.'

'Good for you,' answered Masters. 'I'm pleased to have heard you say it.'

'You wouldn't—couldn't—have expected anything else if you'd known Sally.'

'I've seen a photograph of her.'

'Have you? She looked pretty good, didn't she? But you had to know her to realize what a fantastic girl she was.'

Masters accepted this superficially, mentally putting most of it down to the protestations of a young man in love—notoriously untrustworthy opinions. Something of this attitude must have communicated itself to Dent, who said, 'You're a bit sceptical?'

'Not really. But you *were* going to marry her.'

'So my judgment about her is suspect?'

'I'd expect it to be—a little.'

Dent leaned forward earnestly. 'Let me tell you this, Mr Masters. I'm an only child. And though I think the world of my mother, I'd be the first to admit that she's possessive as far as I'm concerned. I've no illusions about her. She thinks nothing is good enough for me. Nor *anybody*. Ever since I've been old enough to think about marriage, I've expected to have a battle royal with Mother about whichever girl I asked to marry me. I knew—really knew—that if I presented the most noble, beautiful creature that ever lived, as my future wife, mother would be critical. And would try to stop it.'

'Go on, Mr Dent.'

'Mother didn't try to stop my engagement to Sally. Every girl I'd brought home before she came along had been wrong for me. For a variety of reasons. Mother nosed out imperfections in dress, manners, looks, speech, family, character—the lot. But never with Sally. In fact, she encouraged the engagement. Sang Sally's praises to me. Said how clever, beautiful, gay and kind she was. What a wonderful wife and mother she'd make. And believe me, Chief Inspector, any girl whom I wished to marry who could make my mother say what she did, must have been just about as perfect as they come in every respect.'

'You've made your point, Mr Dent,' Masters said. 'And I might as well say that I've heard much the same about Miss Bowker from other people. But I also got the impression that she was a spirited young lady.'

'What d'you mean by that?'

'That I have heard Miss Bowker was very much at home with men and evoked a great amount of respect and admiration from them.'

'Oh yes. Every chap I knew went crackers about her.'

'But her own sex were not always quite so unstinting in their praise of her.'

Dent flushed. 'I don't know what you've heard, but it must be sour grapes.'

'Not entirely, Mr Dent. To be fair, I've heard only one person openly critical—and that taken alone would, I'm sure, be a bad case of sour grapes. But I heard from an independent source that Miss Bowker's very open way with men tended to queer the pitch for other women . . .'

'Good lord! That's impossible. Unless . . .'

'Unless what, Mr Dent?'

Dent reddened. 'I was going to say that nobody could possibly give you that idea unless it was Clara Breese.'

'It wasn't Miss Breese. She has never mentioned the matter to us, but what we did hear about her case—from a third party—seems to substantiate our information. Miss Bowker did, I believe, replace Miss Breese in your affections?'

'I suppose she did, in a way. But before he gets married a man can change his girl friends, can't he?'

'I think it is generally held to be a good thing, Mr Dent. And the choice was yours entirely—if it was your choice.'

'What d'you mean by that?'

'Did you take the decision to break your friendship with Miss Breese and to start one with Miss Bowker, or did Miss Bowker intrude or come between you and Miss Breese with the intention of taking her place?'

Dent jumped to his feet. He looked angrily at Masters. 'Sally's been dead less than a week, and you're here suggesting . . .'

'Suggesting nothing, Mr Dent. Asking. Please sit down. It's not uncommon for one girl to fancy what another's got and go after it with malice aforethought. If I may say so, you're not a bad catch for a girl. You're young, good looking, a professional man with tremendous prospects ahead of you both from your own work and a likely inheritance. These things count in a materialistic world, Mr Dent.'

'Meaning that Sally was marrying me for what she could get?'

'Not exactly. But the ending of your friendship with Miss Breese was not of that young lady's making. Or to her liking. She's been moping ever since, Mr Dent.'

'So?'

'So she was given the push, Mr Dent. By you. And I want to know if Miss Bowker was not only the reason for it, but if she was also responsible for it. Please tell me.'

Dent looked stubborn.

'Well, Mr Dent?'

'The choice—if it was a choice—was mine.'

'What does that mean, exactly?'

'Sally and I just came together naturally.'

'You mean you did nothing to assist the gravitation?'

'There was no need to, I tell you. When two people— what's the popular phrase?—are made for each other, these things happen of their own accord.'

'I understand. Now, let's get back to last Saturday. Miss Bowker lunched at home at one o'clock—to the best of your knowledge?'

'That's right.'

'What were you doing during the morning?'

'Tinkering with the car, mostly.'

'And what else?'

'I read the paper. I always read it more fully on Saturday and Sunday than the rest of the week. I had coffee with my parents.'

'Here?'

'Yes. And I went out with Dad for our usual lunchtime drink.'

'You had made no arrangement to meet Miss Bowker?'

'Not in the morning. I never did. Saturday morning was what Sally used to call her Dorcas morning. It was the only time in the week when she had time to do all the things there are to be done in a home besides her visits to the doctor and the clinic when they fell due.'

'Good enough. But after lunch?'

'We always met in the afternoon. We were getting ready to be married, you know. That day we were looking over a house we thought we might buy.'

'Just one?'

'We'd viewed a lot. But this one was the one we thought we liked, so we were paying a second visit. We were being very thorough about it, as you can imagine.'

'Miss Bowker liked the house?'

'Very much. So did I, but I wanted to make sure it was structurally sound before we made up our minds. I'm an architect by profession, so I could do the survey to my own satisfaction.'

'How long were you there? At this house?'

'I picked Sally up at half-past two. We got back here about five.'

'Here?'

'It's a habit we got into after Sally developed diabetes. On Saturdays we always came here for tea and supper.'

Masters sat silent for a moment. Green appeared lost in thought. Sally Bowker had spent her last five or six hours of normal life in this house. It meant that whoever was present during that time would have to be questioned. 'It became a habit, you say?' Masters asked.

'Yes. It was the only night when I could be sure of seeing Sally, so Mum changed her supper-party night to Saturday.'

'Changed, Mr Dent? When from?'

'Sorry. What I meant was that the parent birds used to entertain on any old night at one time, but because of Sally,

83

Mum stabilized it on Saturday nights. They became a sort of "at home" function with her.'

'Purely on Miss Bowker's account? That was very considerate of your mother.'

'She is considerate—was—where Sally was concerned. She looked after her, you know. The menu and the drinks were always chosen with an eye to what was best for Sally.'

'Didn't that become a little difficult? With other guests to consider?'

'No problem as far as I heard.'

'Your mother knew enough about your fiancée's condition to be able to cope satisfactorily?'

'Not about her condition. She had no medical knowledge that I know of.'

'But she coped.'

'Food was never a problem. Mother was a dietitian.'

'Was?'

'Before she married. She trained before the war. Then during the war she became one of the first area consultants for the school's meals service. The system was introduced at that time and, as I understand it, dietitians being few and far between, mother got a fairly important job—her war service, in fact.'

'Has she done any active professional work since?'

'No. She was already married, and as soon as the war was over and Dad came back, she had me.'

'That's a quarter of a century ago. She'd be a bit rusty now, I expect. However, that's beside the point. She took good care of Miss Bowker.'

'I've told you what Mum thought of Sally. And she proved it often enough. Why, only on Saturday night—well, it was at teatime, actually, when we were all discussing the house we'd been to look over—Dad said that he would give me a thousand pounds to add to the deposit so that the mortgage wouldn't have to be quite so big, and Mum turned to Sally and said, "If Brian's getting a thousand to help pay for the house, I'll give *you* five hundred to help furnish it." '

'That was extremely generous.'

'It certainly was.'

'A spontaneous gesture of affection?'

'Absolutely. Sally had said that she thought the only major work to be done would be in the kitchen. She said she would want to modernize it, make it labour-saving with all these units and gadgets, and Mum—who's a great one in that line herself—simply said she would provide the money. That shows you what she thought of Sally.'

'And what did your father think of her?' Masters asked.

Brian Dent said simply, 'I believe he looked on Sally as the daughter he would have liked for himself.'

Masters relit his pipe. 'Who else was at supper with you on Saturday night?'

'Just one other couple. Friends of Dad's. Alderman and Mrs Bancroft. They're decent bodies. Not all that old.'

'Did Miss Bowker know them?'

'Oh, yes. They knew her parents pretty well in the old days.'

Masters got to his feet. 'I'll have to speak to them and your parents.'

'You can see Mum and Dad now.'

Masters looked at his watch. Then: 'I'd like to meet them. But I'm a bit pushed for time.' Green stared in surprise. Masters hadn't mentioned he was in a hurry. 'Can I just say hallo and perhaps arrange a meeting for a little later on. I must get back into town and we let our car go on some other business.'

'In that case, the nearest way to where they're snoozing is through the kitchen,' Dent said. 'I'll lead the way.'

They followed him. Masters could see how right Brian Dent had been when he said his mother was keen on modern kitchens. This room could have been photographed for the visual of a glossy advertisement. Pale blue units with working surfaces, double sink unit, refrigerator, deep freeze, Bendix, many-clocked electric cooker, infrared grill, Miele dish washer . . .

Through the kitchen to a small lobby; out under the car port and left round the back of the house on to a flagged terrace half as big as a tennis court. Below this, cut out of the lawn, a swimming pool the same size, lined in blue tiles giving the water a Mediterranean invitation. Mrs Dent was in a candy-striped sun suit, lying at ease in a garden swing-lounge, protected from the direct heat by a scallop-edged shade. She wore sun glasses, giving herself a Garboesque anonymity. Masters didn't like it. He preferred to see people's eyes. Dent senior was lying out in a cane chaise-longue. He was wearing sandals, a pair of navy-blue Cal-preta shorts and a wide-brimmed hat made out of canary-yellow terry towelling.

'Chief Inspector Masters and Inspector Green,' Brian said.

Harry Dent said, without getting up, 'You've had a long chat. You're not suspecting Brian of harming Sally are you?'

'That's a question I can't answer,' Masters replied.

'You what?' Masters could see why Hook had described Harry Dent as an old blowhard. His question was an attack in defence of his son. Intended to crush opposition. It had little effect. Masters said, 'I can't eliminate anybody until the guilt has been squarely placed on one person's shoulders.'

'Maybe. But our Brian . . .'

'Was the last to see her alive, Mr Dent. But that doesn't necessarily mean I think he killed her.'

86

'I should bloody well hope not.'

'But I must consider him, just as I must consider you.'

'Me? Now look here . . .' He half rose in his chair.

'And Mrs Dent and everybody connected with Miss Bowker.'

'Don't worry, Dad,' Brian said. 'Everybody's got to go through the hoop on these occasions.'

'But we loved Sally,' Mrs Dent protested.

'I'm sure you did,' Masters answered. 'That's why I'm counting on you to help. Can I call on you later to talk things over?'

'Oh, dear. Must you?'

'Why not now?' Dent asked. 'Get it over with.'

'Because I'm in a hurry to get to another appointment, Mr Dent. Otherwise I could think of nothing nicer than to sit here beside your very lovely pool and talk to you. But I'm afraid it will have to be nine o'clock tonight.'

'That's what you think. I'm not . . .'

His wife cut in: 'Don't be silly, Harry. We must co-operate with the police.'

'That's all very well, Cora, but Saturday night!'

'Is our night for entertaining.' She turned to Masters. 'We weren't, of course, expecting guests tonight, but now you and the other officer are coming it will seem almost as if we were getting back to normal again. Poor Sally! We shall all miss her so much—not just Brian. But we can't hide ourselves away because she died. Life must go on, mustn't it, Mr Masters?'

'Indeed it must, ma'am.'

'There you are, you see, Harry.'

Harry Dent grunted and pulled his towelling cap lower over his eyes. His son said to Masters, 'I'll run you into town if you like.'

'I should be very grateful.'

When they left the E-type at the town centre Green said: 'What's all this about an appointment?'

'I haven't got one. But I want to get to a chemist's shop before they shut.'

Green grunted and stepped out alongside Masters, glancing at his reflection in shop windows as he went. He decided the Palm Beach suiting looked very smart on him. He hoped the hot weather lasted.

5 |

Green said to the girl behind the medicines counter, 'We're police. We'd like to see the pharmacist.'

She left them without a word. In a moment a middle-aged man appeared from behind a frosted-glass dispensing screen. He was bespectacled and bald, with greying side patches of dark hair neatly brushed. He looked nervous, questioning, as if expecting bad news. Masters guessed it cost him quite an effort to approach them and speak.

'I'm the pharmacist. Frane. I own the shop.'

'We'd like a few words with you in private,' Green said.

Frane looked even more perturbed. 'Of course. If you'd come round the end of the counter.' The girl was standing by, saying nothing, but looking slightly apprehensive. Masters smiled at her and said, 'Don't worry. We only want some information.' She smiled back at him, gratefully. Frane heard the message. He seemed a little more cheerful as he ushered them into the dispensary.

'We're investigating the death of a diabetic girl, Mr Frane.' Masters explained.

'Oh, yes.'

'You've heard about the case?'

'The one there was an inquest on a few days ago?'

'That's right.'

'I didn't have anything to do with supplying her insulin.'

'No. We realize that. All we're here for is to get some information about insulin and the amounts the patient takes. You see, Mr Frane, all the talk about diabetes and its treatment is way above our heads, so we've come to an expert to help us out.'

'Oh, I see.'

'Will you be willing to answer a few questions?'

'If I can. Yes.'

'Thank you. Now the dead girl was using Rapitard insulin.'

'Rapitard? Yes. That's the neutral insulin with the bluey-green colour code. Easy to remember, Rapitard. Both labels have very similar colour triangles.'

'Perhaps you would explain? Colour triangles?'

'Let me see, now, there are how many different types of insulin? Soluble, protamine, globine, isophane ...' He counted on his fingers as he went through them. 'Nine. Yes, nine types. And every type is designated by a different colour.'

'Rapitard is bluey-green?'

'Correct. But there are two strengths of all those nine. Forty units per mil and eighty units per mil. And strengths, too, have to be colour-coded.'

'I see.'

'The colour for U forty is blue, and for U eighty, green—on all types. So what we do is to divide the square packing label into two triangles. The bottom left triangle is coloured either blue or green to denote the strength. The top right triangle has its individual colour to denote the type. Well, like I said, Rapitard is easy to remember, because its own colour is bluey-green, while its strength colours are blue and green.'

Green looked a little lost and Masters wasn't quite sure he'd got it, but he said to Frane, 'That's very clear. Now to talk about the amounts in the syringe at each injection.'

'Very small. Very small. But, of course, they differ with every patient according to his or her needs.'

'Do they?'

'Most certainly.'

'I see. So you can't tell me how much this girl would

inject each time?'

'Not unless I knew how much . . .'

'She got four ten mil phials to last her exactly four weeks.'

'Ah! Well in that case . . .' Frane took a pencil from the breast pocket of his white coat and drew a pad towards him. 'Forty mils for four weeks means ten mils a week means ten-sevenths of a mil a day.' He looked up. 'Rapitard is a combination of quick and slow acting insulins. Its effects last something like ten or twelve hours so it's usually given in two injections a day.'

'That's right. The dead girl had one before breakfast and one before supper.'

'So she had ten-fourteenths at each injection which is point seven of a mil.'

'And how big's a mil?'

Frane picked up a ruler and marked off a centimetre with his two thumbs. 'A cubic c.c.'

'That's pretty small.'

'It might appear so. But in fact it's quite big so I would say. Her doctor must have been giving her U forty.'

'How d'you know?'

'An active young woman like her would need a good dose but not a massive one. One mil of U forty contains forty units. Point seven would contain . . .' He did a quick sum on the pad. '. . . twenty-eight units; and that would be about what I'd expect her to have.'

Masters took from his pocket the slip of paper Dr Sisson had given him. 'Can I buy ten mils of Rapitard from you? Against this?'

Frane read the note and nodded.

'And a one mil syringe?'

'A BS 1619?'

'If that's the standard?'

'It is. Fitted with Luer needles.'

'I'll take that.'

Frane went to the back of the dispensary and got the goods. 'You're not going to practise injecting yourselves?' he asked.

'Not bloody likely,' Green replied. 'I've had enough jabs in my time without any experiments.'

'Good. Is that all?'

'You've been most helpful over the insulin. I wonder, could you give me some information about emetics. I know there's ipecac, of course, but I seem to remember that it has a very bitter taste.'

'Not the syrup, so much. You can buy that at any chemist's. And though it is an emetic, it's usually used for coughs. An emetic dose would have to be very large. Anything up to an ounce and a half.'

'What other forms are there?'

'You can get it in Dover's Powders and various cough linctuses, but I don't think they'd work as emetics.'

'Is the syrup bought very often?' Masters asked.

'Fairly often. Sales are growing as a matter of fact. You see, certain authorities are now recommending that it should be kept in every household where there are children, so that if a child eats or drinks a poisonous substance, there's a dose of ipecac handy. It is hoped that a large dose will make the child vomit before it even reaches hospital. If it does, it's half the battle in putting them right.'

'Are there any other forms—more concentrated?'

Frane grimaced. 'There's the fluidextract. That's the strong solution—fourteen times as strong as the syrup—from which the syrup is made.'

'Is that freely available?'

'There's nothing to prevent a chemist selling it, but not many would stock it. Very few make up their own syrups these days; and I think if somebody were to ask me for fluidextract I should look sideways at them.'

'Why?'

'Because it's so bitter and potent. One or two drops could make somebody very ill. I tasted a little when I was an apprentice. Only a little, mark you.'

'What happened?'

'I was that sick I thought I'd have flung my pluck up. And the taste! The memory of it's enough for me. You know how a bitter lemon tastes harsh and draws your mouth? Multiply it a thousand times and you get ipecac fluidextract.'

Masters stood silent for a moment. Frane went on: 'It's no business of mine, but why questions about emetics?'

'The girl was very sick. I just wondered if she could have been given something to bring it on.'

'Not without her knowing. All the emetics are nasty tasting. Take common salt for instance. Think how hard it would be to disguise an emetic dose of that in anything short of a gallon of soup. It would be very difficult indeed to make anybody sick without them knowing.'

'I see. Thank you. You've been very helpful, Mr Frane.'

'Sorry I couldn't do more for you.'

Masters smiled at the chemist, so sure of himself now that he was on his own ground. 'You've done a great deal. All information—even if only negative—is useful. It stops us chasing hares and wandering off the main track. We're grateful for even those small mercies.'

'Yes, I suppose so. It all saves work. And talking of work, I've got prescriptions to make up.'

'Of course. We'll see ourselves out.'

Green said, 'That's a new one on me.'

'What is?'

' "I thought I'd have flung my pluck up." '

'New to me, too. But descriptive—if a little inelegant.'

'Did you get anything from him—other than the information about the insulin?'

'Perhaps. We shall have to see.'

They turned into the Bristol. Tea was served in the lounge. Green poured. 'D'you think anybody would mind if I took my jacket off?' he asked, glancing round at several other people all engaged with toasted tea cakes and scones.

'Not so long as you haven't got braces on.'

Green sat down in his shirt sleeves. The heat had not curbed his appetite. It was some minutes before his mouth was disengaged enough to make conversation possible. He then said, 'Who've we got? Breese, Nurse Ward, Brian Dent. Anybody else?'

'Why Dent?'

'The pass key. You didn't ask about it.'

'You think it's important?'

'Maybe.'

'Dent senior could have got at it as easily as his son.'

'Maybe he could. But you can't suspect him.'

'Why not?'

'He liked the lass.'

'So did Brian. Enough to want to marry her. And his mother. She liked her enough to give her five hundred pounds.'

'Yes. But you don't give two people a couple of presents like a thousand quid and five hundred quid at tea time and then start bumping them off an hour or two later. So you can't suspect the parents. It wouldn't make sense.'

'Perhaps not. Though I'd say it depends on the way you look at it. I wonder if Hill and Brant have had any luck?'

'I hope so.' Green wiped his mouth and mopped his forehead with his handkerchief. 'Otherwise we're in a bit of a hole. I'm beginning to think that I've never been so fogbound as I am in this case.'

'Oh, surely!' Masters said, handing his cup over for a refill.

'It's right. In fact I'm beginning to think the girl wasn't seen off at all. She just died. Have you thought of that?'

'I have.'

'And I'll bet what that chemist had to say made you think you were right. No chance of making her puke artificially. So she just took ill and died.'

'She *was* feeling sick, *did* vomit. *And* her insulin was useless. *And* she died because of it.'

'I know. The two sides balance out.'

'They don't. Her death is a positive fact. The fact that emetics are difficult to disguise is a negative point. She may not have been given an emetic. It was just a thought of mine.'

'Quite a reasonable one,' said Green graciously. 'But how about this for a theory? Are you listening?'

'With bated breath.' Green was always anxious that nobody should miss his pearls. They were cast so rarely.

'That carrying-case of hers. There was room for two bottles of insulin.'

Masters nodded.

'She must have taken two with her.'

'Because there were two compartments in the case?'

'No. Because her old stock was due to last until Saturday evening. So she'd take the last dose out of one bottle just before supper that night at the Dents', and she'd have the new bottle with her as well just in case of accidents. Right?'

'By the lord Harry I'd overlooked that.'

Green smirked. 'Well then, if the new bottle was mucked about with, why not the old bottle, too? That would mean she had useless insulin before supper. Without the insulin to counteract it the food made her feel sick. When she got home she started the new bottle. That was duff, too, so she grew worse and died. No emetic needed.'

Masters began to fill his pipe. Green waited expectantly for comments. Masters kept him in expectation for some moments before saying, 'You may be right, at that. Sisson should be able to tell us.'

Green, slightly disappointed, said, 'You don't think much of the idea.'

'I certainly do. So much so, in fact, that I shall proceed using your theory as a fact. It must have happened as you say. It's a natural. But! And here you'll remember better than I do what Sisson said about insulin-hunger—*it takes a hell of a long time to come on.* Now, Sally Bowker would be perfectly normal until seven or half-past at night. Then she had a useless injection. By eleven o'clock—less than four hours later—she wouldn't be far gone. Nowhere near approaching a coma. So I still think she was given something that positively upset her, as well as having her insulin rendered useless. And I think the two combined killed her, where only one or the other might not have done.'

'So my theory doesn't help us on.'

'It does, tremendously. It irons out one of my mental reservations. But I don't think it will stand alone.'

Green squeezed the teapot, draining the last trickle from the leaves. Masters knew he felt that his theory should have been received with more acclaim. But what the hell! Green was paid for it. What more did he want? Medals?

The two sergeants came into the lounge. 'Order another pot, quick,' Green demanded.

'So's you can have it?' Hill asked. 'I like that!'

Brant sat down. 'Any joy?' Masters asked him.

'Nothing.'

'On either of them?'

'We got a little on Breese to help confirm her story, and

nothing to show she was lying. There's not a sausage on Nurse Ward.'

'Now where do we go for honey?' Green asked.

Hill joined them. 'Why? What's up? Case fallen through or something?' he said.

'Or something,' Green answered. 'We can't get a lead.'

Brant, through a mouthful of sandwich, said, 'So we've started giving up in less than twenty-four hours now, have we?' He looked inquiringly at Masters, who shook his head slowly.

'Apart from seeing the Dents tonight, what are we going to do?' asked Green.

'I think I'll go and see Hook,' Masters said. 'If somebody could drive me there.'

Hook wasn't at the Station. Masters and Hill found him at his home. He welcomed them warmly. Asked Masters for an account of his activities and conclusions, and declared himself satisfied, though it was fairly obvious from his manner that he had hoped for more startling revelations even at this early date.

'What I really came for, sir, was to talk about the post-mortem findings,' Masters said.

'You've got the report. Slight traces of alcohol. No signs of any toxic substance in the body. No signs of stomach irritation. Serious lack of mineral salts, chiefly potassium, due to dehydration brought about by excessive vomiting.'

'Who did the post-mortem?'

'The pathologist at the hospital. He's not a fool. He's an able man.'

'I'm sure he is, but I've known cases where sometimes some indication has been missed because the doctor wasn't specifically looking for it. For instance, did he specifically look for traces of ipecac? Can he definitely state there were none?'

Hook scratched his ear. 'See what you mean. He'd explore for every poison he knew, but he might not test for emetics. That what you mean?'

Masters nodded.

'Best thing to do is ring him up and ask. Hang on a bit. I'll call you to the phone when I get him. Name's Heatherington-Blowers. Likes both barrels.'

'I'll remember.'

Hook went to the telephone in the hall. Masters heard him dial and speak. Then he reappeared. 'He's on now.'

Masters picked up the phone. 'I'm interested in emetics, Dr Heatherington-Blowers. I was wondering whether you had tested for them in the post mortem.'

'No. I'm inclined to think it would be a waste of time to do so, Chief Inspector.'

'Could you tell me why, sir?'

'Because emetics are not usually metabolized. You know what that means?'

'Absorbed into the living substance of the body?'

'Roughly that. Of course some substances which are metabolized bring on nausea, but an emetic as such is usually an irritant to the gastric mucosa—stomach linings—to put it in layman's terms. That's what causes the vomiting. And if the vomiting is severe the emetic, being unmetabolized, is discharged from the body in the vomit. But had you any particular emetic in mind?'

'I only know ipecac.'

'Yes. That's the most likely, but the dose would have to be a big one, and so I'm certain I'd have noticed if it had been given. You see, ipecac in a dose large enough to act as an emetic would also cause diarrhoea, and there was no sign of that.'

Masters paused before replying. He was so long silent

that Heatherington-Blowers asked, 'Are you still there, Chief Inspector?'

'Yes, sir. Thinking.'

'About what?'

'You said that an emetic would be discharged in the vomit?'

'Yes, almost certainly and in this case, almost entirely.'

'Did you test the vomit by any chance?'

'No. I wasn't asked to, nor was I given a sample.'

'But if she had been given an emetic there would be traces of it in the vomit?'

'I should say so. But you're too late. There is no sample. Never was as far as I know.'

'There may be, sir.'

'I understood the girl had vomited into the lavatory basin—however many times there was emesis—and had managed to flush it away. Very plucky young woman she must have been, because the amount she got rid of must have left her very weak.'

'She certainly was plucky, sir, because we have found a floorcloth. It was hanging on the U bend behind the lavatory pan. And from the smell of it, she used it to wipe up vomit.'

'You mean she may have splashed the floor and had enough hold on herself to clean it up?'

'That's my belief, sir.'

'You may be right. Everybody feels a bit better—if only temporarily—after being sick. She may have mopped up during a short period of relief.'

'Could that floorcloth be tested, sir?'

'Yes. I suppose so. I'm not a forensic expert, you know, but Superintendent Hook could get it done, I feel sure. He'll know the nearest forensic laboratory. Bristol, Birmingham maybe. Ask him.'

'It couldn't be done here?'

'You mean you'd like me to try.'

'If possible.'

'In that case, my best bet is to ask the bacteriologist to assist. When can we have the floorcloth?'

'Within half an hour.'

'It's Saturday evening. Wouldn't tomorrow morning do? There'll be a host of qualitative and quantitative analyses to be carried out.'

And with that Masters had to be content. He promised to send the cloth to the hospital in good time for an early start.

At dinner, Green asked, 'So even Heatherington-Blowers has given you the thumbs-down sign, has he?'

Masters was waiting for a steak. It was being grilled by a chef who was tumbling it under a lighted gas jet at the end of the dining-room. He said, peevishly, 'It takes a season to do a bit of meat. I ordered a quarter of an hour ago.'

'It's a thick one,' Hill answered. 'Black as the ace of spades on the outside and bloody inside. Me, I prefer minute steaks, thin fillets, not rump or porterhouse uncooked and looking like the result of a pile-up on the M1.'

'Shut up. I've got to eat that.'

'Not "got to", Chief.'

'Never mind. You know what I mean.'

The steak arrived.

'Now you've got it,' Green said, 'perhaps you'll tell us whether the pathologist was hopeful or pessimistic.'

Masters helped himself to mushrooms. 'He didn't say.'

'Judging from your attitude, he didn't have to. You're not hopeful. You're crabby.'

'Sorry. Perhaps I was. But I'm beginning to think I've

no reason to be.' He turned to Hill and Brant.'I don't suppose Sally Bowker's handbag or that little aluminium box have been tested for prints. I'd like that done tonight.'

'We've all handled the box,' Green pointed out.

'I know. Pity. But it can be tested.'

'What if she's more than one handbag?' Hill asked.

'Try them all. And get a set of her own prints for comparison. There should be plenty of sets about.'

Green said, 'You're letting that bloody steak get cold—if it was ever hot through.'

Masters forked a piece into his mouth. 'It's a lovely steak. Just lovely.'

They set out for the Dent house at a quarter to nine.

Masters asked Brant, 'How long is it going to take you to get those prints?'

'Half an hour.'

'Right. Come back here as soon as you've got them, and wait outside. We may be longer than you, but I'll make it as short as possible.'

He and Green walked up to the Dents' front door. It was still full daylight and warm. But not uncomfortably so, as it had been earlier in the day. The night-scented stock was perfuming the air beside the path, and the Livingstone daisies had closed up for the night. A midsummer evening. Not the time to be thinking of murder and hell-brews. Masters felt a surge of distaste for his job. He wondered what Green was thinking about.

Brian Dent opened the door and showed them into the same sitting-room. Harry Dent was in dark grey trousers and a cream linen jacket. Mrs Dent was on the sofa with her feet up. She made no attempt to rise to greet them. Masters eyed her well. He felt she ran true to type. Blue-rinsed hair, an overpowdered face with sharp features.

Shrewd eyes with wrinkled peripheries. Large dangling earrings in yellow metal and a long chain of the same material round her neck. The dress was thin wool—blue—cut square at the neck, with short sleeves. Her hands showed her age. On the third finger of her left hand she wore three rings. The nails were red and too long for Masters' liking. Her stockings had the modern, anaemic white sheen; her shoes were blue suede with a large bow at the instep. She offered her hand. Masters would have preferred not to take it, but he did so, bowing slightly more in the effort to get down to it than out of courtesy.

'Sit down, Mr Masters. We have waited for coffee until you came. Brian, darling, bring in the trolley.'

When they had all been served, Masters began, 'I'd like to learn exactly what Miss Bowker did and ate between teatime last Saturday and the time when she left here. But first one other minor point which concerns both you gentlemen.'

'What's that?' Harry Dent said.

'The master key to Wye House. It is, I understand, in your possession.'

They both stared at him for a moment. He watched them closely. They didn't appear to be following the drift. 'Anybody with a master key to the block could have entered Miss Bowker's flat at will.'

'What for?' Brian Dent asked.

'To doctor her insulin, maybe.'

'Are you accusing us of entering her flat?' Harry said angrily.

'No. I merely want to satisfy myself that the key was not used.'

'You must see that a spare key could be important,' Green added.

Brian Dent looked at his father, who said, 'Our key wasn't used, either by Brian, myself or anybody else.'

'How d'you know?' Green asked him.

'For one thing, we haven't access to it.'

'Your firm is the agent.'

'We own the block. We manage it for ourselves. But that's not the point. Our firm is divided up into watertight compartments. Brian here is the architect and does property surveys. I'm the auctioneer. Anything for sale, from a second-hand bath to a thousand-acre farm, is my pigeon. Property management is another department, and neither Brian nor myself ever hears about it except at board meetings. I don't know where pass keys are kept, but I'd guess they're in the property-department safe to which neither of us has access.'

Masters looked at Brian. 'Do you confirm that?'

'Certainly. When the police wanted the key last Monday night we had to roust out Joe Little, the property manager, to get it for us.'

Masters turned to Green. Green said, 'That sounds fair enough—for the moment.'

'What the hell d'you mean?' Harry Dent growled. 'For the moment?'

'It means we're taking your word for it unless and until we have reason to think otherwise.'

Dent was about to reply, but his wife prevented him. 'Now, Harry. Don't lose your temper. These gentlemen are only doing their job.'

'Maybe they are. But it's obviously so bloody silly to think Brian or myself killed Sally.'

Masters said, 'Somebody did. Can you suggest who, Mr Dent?'

'No, I can't. If I knew who it was I'd scrag them myself.'

'That's what I thought. You were fond of her.'

It was a statement. Dent didn't deny it. Masters waited a moment and then said, 'Mr Brian told us of Miss

Bowker's activities in the afternoon up to the time he brought her here for tea, at which time, I understand, you both made them very generous offers of help with the house they intended to buy.'

'Oh, he shouldn't have mentioned that,' Mrs Dent said.

'Why not, ma'am?'

'It was a little family secret.'

'Maybe. But it showed me very vividly the regard in which you held Miss Bowker. And that is of great interest to me.'

Mrs Dent gave him a little smile. He was impressed by the quality of her false teeth.

'Now. Tea. What was on the menu?' he asked.

'Very ordinary. A plate of sandwiches—cucumber I think. But Sally didn't have any of those, poor dear. She just had biscuits. Semi-sweet, you know. Thin arrowroot and Marie. That sort of thing. You see, I knew what she could eat, and with her parents not being near to look after her, I took care to see she got the right food—at any rate when she was here.'

'It does you credit, ma'am. No cakes with fillings or icing that might have upset her?'

'Dear me, no. A Victoria sponge with raspberry jam in the middle. But she didn't have any, although she could have. It wouldn't have done her any harm.'

Masters turned to the men. 'You both ate everything without feeling any ill effects?'

'I didn't touch the biscuits,' Harry Dent said. 'Never do, except with cheese.'

'I had one or two off Sally's plate,' Brian said. 'She said mother had overloaded her a bit.'

'Oh, Brian, I didn't. She could have left the ones she didn't want.'

'Of course, Mum. Sal was only joking.'

'Can we move on a bit? What happened after tea?'

'Sally and I washed up,' Brian answered. 'Then while mother got dinner ready, we went in for a swim.'

'In your own pool?'

'Yes. Here, I say. You don't think the chlorine in the water upset Sal, do you?'

'Why? Was it strong?' Green asked.

'No. Not very.'

'I'm sorry to be so pernickety,' Masters continued, 'but let us go through step by step. You washed up in the kitchen?'

'Yes.'

'When did you decide to swim?'

'I don't know, really. We do it so often.'

'It's become a ritual?'

'Yes.'

'But Miss Bowker would need a swimsuit.'

'She always carried one at weekends—in her bag. A wispy bit of a thing. Bikini.'

'Oh, Brian, it was beautiful,' Mrs Dent said. 'It was thin cotton in one of those soft, deep-plunging styles without any pads or bones. It made her look so young and lovely. It was turquoise and green and went so well with her fair complexion. And with the colour of the water in the pool, too. It crumpled up into no more than a handful, and then sprang out without a crease. I always admired it and wished I dare wear one like it.'

'She certainly looked marvellous in it,' Brian said.

'Where did she change?' asked Masters.

'In the downstairs cloakroom. Mother used to put towels in there . . .'

Mrs Dent interrupted, 'It sounds awful, giving them the downstairs cloakroom as a changing-room, but honestly, Chief Inspector, you should see the mess they make of everything. They just come out of the water and traipse through the house, dripping water on the carpets and polished floors. I had to put a stop to it. And besides, the cloakroom is very handy. Just next to the kitchen, and the floor in there doesn't matter because it can be mopped.'

'Very wise, ma'am,' Masters said. He turned to Harry Dent. 'And you, sir, where were you at this time?'

'Watching the box. I wanted to see the last half-hour of the Test, and I just sat there until seven, when I went up to change before Alderman and Mrs Bancroft came.'

'That's very clear. Now, what time did you come out of the pool, Mr Dent?'

'Sally got out about seven. She changed first and gave herself her injection. I came out when she called to say she was clear.'

'I see. Now, her injection. She always carried a box with her syringe and bottles I believe?'

'In her bag. With the bikini and the usual junk you find in women's handbags. Sally always used the sling variety. They seemed to suit her, and they had the capacity she needed.'

'Where did she leave her bag? At the side of the pool?'

Mrs Dent said: 'She always kept it with her, poor dear. It was so important to her.'

'Usually, Mum. But not when we went swimming. She always left it in the cloakroom.'

'Why was that, Mr Dent?' Masters asked. 'So it didn't get splashed?'

'No. Nothing like that. She couldn't have cared less. But she never swam unless it was pretty warm. Dr Sisson told her to be very careful about catching cold. Any infection is about ten times worse in a diabetic than other people, apparently. So, for it to be warm enough for Sally to swim, the flags round the pool had to be hot to the feet. And that's too hot for insulin. She'd never leave her bag on the pool surround or lying out in the sun. She left it in the cool of the cloakroom.'

'I see. Thank you, Mr Dent. So Miss Bowker injected herself. Now, according to my information, that injection should just have finished one phial.'

'That's right,' Mrs Dent said. 'She dropped an empty one into the pedal bin in the kitchen when she went to call Brian.'

Masters thanked her for the information and then asked, 'You sat down for supper at what time?'

'Prompt on half-past seven,' Mrs Dent replied. 'We had to be very strict about times with Sally. She had to have her meal exactly half an hour after her injection.'

'What was on the menu?'

'It was a very ordinary meal.'

'Nonsense, Mum. It was a splendid meal,' Brian Dent exclaimed. He turned to Masters. 'You're wondering whether the meal could have upset Sally?'

'Yes, Mr Dent, I am. I must. She felt sick when you took her home, didn't she?'

'Yes. But it couldn't have been Mother's food. We all ate it. Melon—Sally had glucose on hers. Thin, lean steaks, with no fat. New potatoes which Sally didn't have . . .'

'Why?'

'Because she had her weekly drink on Saturdays and she had to leave some of her calorie and carbohydrate allowance to make up for it.'

'I see. Go on with the menu, please.'

'New carrots and peas. Followed by stewed plums and cream, biscuits and cheese. Sally had no cream.'

'Coffee?'

'Sally had black with saccharin. And her liqueur. The drink I told you about.'

'Liqueur?'

Mrs Dent said, 'Yes, poor lamb. She said that if she was

restricted to one drink a week she might as well have the sort she liked best. She loved liqueurs. Before she became diabetic she always liked liqueur chocolates, didn't she Brian?'

'Yes, Mum.'

'I can always remember the first gift you took her was a box of liqueurs. I remember thinking how sweet it was of you to find out in advance what she really liked.'

Brian coloured as his mother spoke. It obviously embarrassed him. Masters remembered how that afternoon he had said that his mother thought no girl good enough for him. He thought she would obviously make a fool of the lad if he hadn't had enough good sense to stop her.

'What liqueur?' he asked.

'Well, she liked Benedictine most of all,' Mrs Dent answered.

'A very good choice. Did she take Benedictine last Saturday?'

'Unfortunately, no. We'd run out.'

'My fault,' Harry Dent broke in. 'We'd run out of everything except Anisette. I'm responsible for drink and I didn't cotton on that we were so low in liqueurs. You know how it is. You buy whisky and gin regularly, but replenish with liqueurs once in a blue moon. But Sal didn't mind. Said she rather liked it in fact, though it's not to everybody's taste.'

'Did everybody take liqueurs?'

'Only the women. We three men took brandy.'

'And after dinner?'

'We sat round and talked until Sally said she'd like to go home,' said Brian. 'I took her.'

'She didn't eat anything else?'

'Nothing.'

Masters got to his feet. 'Thank you all very much. I think I've got a complete picture. If I haven't I can always get in touch to clear up any points.'

'Has it helped?' Mrs Dent asked.

Masters smiled. 'Who can tell, ma'am? I firmly believe that everything helps in some way. I'm wrong at times, but one thing I can say is that I've never been successful without getting the whole picture. Perhaps it's because I haven't got a lot of imagination, or I can't visualize what I don't actually see.'

Harry Dent said, 'Don't try to fool yourself—or us. We've heard of you, you know. I reckon I wouldn't mind having you in business with me.'

'I'll remember that, Mr Dent. Policemen retire early, you know. When the time comes I might be glad of a job.'

When they were in the car Green commented, 'Well, that appeared to be all square and above board. But I don't think you pressed that key issue half hard enough.'

'Sorry. Why didn't you step in?'

Green shrugged. It was now dark and the gesture was lost on Masters, who said to Hill, 'What about prints?'

'About six sets on the syringe case. All male except Bowker's.'

'And the handbags?'

'Male and female on all of them.'

'Did you find one with a turquoise and green bikini in it?'

'Yes.'

'That's the one. We'll try to identify the prints tomorrow.'

'That's not going to give us much time for a lie-in,' Hill said.

6

Hill and Brant had delivered the floorcloth to the hospital pathology laboratory and were back at the Bristol before Masters and Green came down for breakfast on Sunday. When he arrived, Masters asked, 'Did they say what time the result of the test would be ready?'

'Nobody there *to* ask,' Hill replied.

'Then who did you give it to?'

'A lab technician. He said Heatherington-Blowers and Bruce, the bacteriologist, would begin work about half-past nine.'

Green said, 'I'm ordering a mixed grill. I've never been in a pub before where they actually advertise a mixed grill for breakfast. I've concocted my own now and again. You know, ordered bacon, eggs, kidneys, sausages, the lot, all on one plate. I wonder whether their idea of a mixed grill will be the same as mine.'

'They'll probably put a lamb chop in it and bring you the mint sauce,' said Brant. 'Mint sauce is lovely at breakfast time.'

'The one you're talking about and the one I won't get'll make two.'

'As it looks like being another hot day,' Masters said, 'I'll have orange juice and boiled eggs. Meanwhile I could do with a cup of coffee.'

Hill poured. 'Those prints . . .' he began.

'Yes?'

'How will we identify them?'

'Perhaps you won't be able to just yet. But separate out Sally Bowker's, mine and the Inspector's. Dr Sisson will have handled the carrying-case, so get his by going and asking for them. Then go to the Station and ask who went to the flat, and get theirs. After that, see what you've got left.'

'That's a load of mullarkey,' Green exclaimed. 'Talk about shots in the dark!'

Masters' eggs arrived in a double cup. As he took the top off one he said, 'You don't think the prints are important?'

'No. And neither do you. You're just casting around, seeing what you can dredge up.'

'This is a very good egg. Free range, I should think. And done just right. White hard, yolk soft. You were saying?'

'That you haven't got a clue.'

'Oh yes I have. Several.' The mixed grill appeared. 'Now that's a fine foundation for a man to go to work on. No mutton, I see. But a nice helping of the offal you swore you'd never touch again. I assure you, as far as this case is concerned I know exactly where I'm going. The only fly in the ointment will be proof. Certain facets of that may present difficulties. The trouble is that I shall have to sit back and wait for some time. So I shall arm myself with several of the more lurid Sunday papers and retire to the garden for an hour or so.'

'What are you trying to do?' Green asked. 'Boost morale among the troops faced with a hopeless situation?'

Hill and Brant said nothing. Masters had surprised them too often ⌐ ⌐ them to doubt his word. Green, who had been more in the swim than they had, was in a stronger position to scoff. But Green had the unhappy knack of scoffing at the wrong things. They knew this very well. They left the table together. When they were out of ear-shot Hill said, 'Do you really think he's got it sewn up?'

'I've never known him say he has when he hasn't.'

'So you think he's sure he knows who it is, but he's short on proof?'

'That's what he says. I'm not going to argue.'

Green was reading the *News of The World*. Masters was attempting a crossword too difficult for him. He put it aside and filled his pipe. Green grunted at some item that he was reading, and put his feet up on a nearby chair. 'D'you think Harry Dent belongs to some club or goes to a particular pub at lunchtime on Sundays?' Masters asked.

Without looking up, Green said, 'How the hell should I know?'

'I want to talk to him privately.'

Green lowered his paper. 'What for?'

'And I want a word with Alderman and Mrs Bancroft.'

Green lit a Kensitas. He blew smoke out of the corner of his mouth and said, 'Now I know you're up the creek. With a fishing-line. You're casting like mad. With little hope of a bite, I reckon.'

'You read your paper for a bit,' Masters suggested. 'And order some coffee. I'll get Bancroft's address from the phone book.'

'Order the coffee as you go through. I'm involved in less mundane things.'

'If you're reading the bits I think you are, they're of the earth, most earthy.'

Over coffee, at which the sergeants joined them, Masters said to Green, 'As you're so immersed in the newspapers, you and Brant can stay here in case Heatherington-Blowers calls. If he does, take a message, or if he particularly wants to speak to me, tell him I hope to be back for lunch, and I'll call him then.'

'Right. You're going to see Bancroft?'

'I've said I'll be there by eleven-fifteen, so Hill and I will be off.'

'You'll get nothing from him except confirmation of last Saturday's menu.'

'The trouble with you is you know what you're going to hear in advance. I don't. I'm continually being surprised. I like it that way.'

'Suits me.'

Masters and Hill passed through the hotel to the car. Hill drove through the almost deserted Sunday streets and made good time round the by-pass to an area of Edwardian houses, still well maintained, and obviously in what the house agents usually call 'a select area'. Bancroft opened the door to them, and Masters felt faintly surprised to find him a man of—at a guess—some years short of fifty. For Masters the term alderman conjured up the justice in fair round belly, with an agate-stone ring on the forefinger; and a nose that rolled its loud diapason after dinner. Bancroft didn't fit the picture. He was a small man, not more than five feet six, but carefully made and well cared for. His hair was greying slightly, but there was a lot of it, brushed neatly. The face was brown, not thin, not fleshy, but handsome with an air of character that allows certain features to be picked out in a crowd as being above the common ruck. His clothes were well pressed, but gave no hint of being Sunday suitish. Masters liked him on sight. 'Come you in and sit you down,' he said. 'I'll call Cordelia. She's picking parsley for the lunchtime potatoes.'

Cordelia was taller than her husband. Not much. And the disparity was not obvious unless looked for. She didn't surprise Masters. Having seen Bancroft, this was the woman he would have expected as his wife. A good figure, just thickening slightly round the beam to indicate she was not quite as young as—without artificial aid—she appeared to be. She wore a pale blue linen skirt and a white pique shirt open at the neck. Masters wondered why all women couldn't buy such simple shoes to enhance their underpinning. He didn't realize that most could probably not afford to do so: that in all forms of female clothing simplicity comes dear and is synonymous with quality.

'I heard from Harry Dent that you would likely be calling,' Bancroft said. 'I'm pleased you have.'

'Why, Mr Bancroft? Have you something you particularly wish to tell me?'

'Good heavens, no.'

'We're as big a pair of scalp hunters as you could hope to find in a day's march, Mr Masters,' Cordelia explained. 'We *like* meeting famous people.'

Masters grinned, delighted at the compliment. He said, but not at all modestly, 'Infamous is what you mean, ma'am. I'm never mentioned except in the same breath as crime. An uncomfortable partnership; and a man's known by the company he keeps.'

'Not necessarily. Not when he overcomes his environment—as we often hear you do.'

'You only get to hear about the good bits. Successes make news. Routine failures don't.'

She laughed. It was a good sound. Musical. 'Sit down and make yourselves comfortable. That's right. In the big chair.'

When they were seated, she asked, 'Can I stay? Or am I to be banished to the kitchen?'

'You'd better stay, Coddy,' Bancroft said. 'I expect the Chief Inspector wants to talk about last Saturday night, and you're far better at remembering details than I am.'

Cordelia settled back in her chair. 'Quite right,' Masters said. 'I'd like to speak to both of you, and it is last Saturday night I'm interested in. And first of all, the meal. Can you remember it?'

'Steak and stewed fruit,' Bancroft said. 'Rather good, I thought.'

'Oh, Ken,' his wife protested. 'Just like a man. It was a

lovely meal. Cora Dent is a wonderful cook, Mr Masters, and she knows how to put on a properly balanced meal. She was catering for a diabetic girl, two middle-aged women with average appetites, two elderly men who eat too much anyway and a young, vigorous man who needs good meals. All at once. And she succeeded admirably. Everybody was beautifully satisfied. And she always manages to get that wonderful effect that you see in coloured photographs when her meals are on the plates. Those little green peas beside the lovely colour of the young carrots. The steak looking just right and every potato exactly the same size, shape and colour, with a little sprinkling of parsley butter on top. That's what I was doing when you came. Trying to achieve the same effect. But I can't do it, no matter how hard I try.'

Kenneth Bancroft said, 'This sounds like a meeting of the selection committee for the local art exhibition.'

'It was certainly a vivid description. Now, what about the rest of the meal?'

Mrs Bancroft confirmed the full menu as described the previous evening by Mrs Dent.

'Did either of you two suffer any ill effects from the meal?'

Cordelia shook her head. 'It was as good and fresh as it could be. Cora is a dietitian, you know. She makes a god of kitchen cleanliness and food storage.'

'I was a bit loose the next day,' Bancroft said. 'I remember saying to you, Coddy . . .'

'Nonsense, Ken. You ate a bowl of stewed prunes for breakfast last Sunday morning because you were too idle to boil yourself an egg.' She turned to Masters. 'He came down so late I'd cleared away an hour before he appeared, so he just had what he could find in the fridge.'

Masters grinned. He took his pipe from his breast pocket where it was wedged, bowl upright, by a white silk handkerchief. 'Do you mind if I smoke?'

She gave him permission. He said, as he rubbed the Warlock Flake, 'What about drinks? Did they upset you?'

'Brandy helps the digestive juices, I find,' Bancroft answered. 'The girls drank some of that pinkish stuff—German Liqueur—not kummel . . .'

'Anisette?'

'That's it.'

'I liked it,' Cordelia said. 'But I don't care for kümmel. I never liked seedy cake when I was a child.'

'Cumin seeds,' her husband said.

'No. Caraway.'

'Never mind, Coddy.'

'Did any of you eat or drink anything else, after supper?'

'The men had more brandy. That's why Kenneth was so late up the next day. But we women had nothing else to drink. Cora and I both had *After Eight* mints, but Sally wouldn't touch them. Sensible child. She knew she'd had her full allowance of carbohydrates or calories or whatever for one day. For ever, I suppose you could say now. It is a shame, Chief Inspector. She was a nice lassie.'

'Somebody didn't think so, Mrs Bancroft.'

'No I was forgetting. You think she was murdered, don't you? It seems impossible to me. We were all laughing and joking over our meal . . .'

Hill said, 'About the meal, ma'am. Didn't you have any wine at table?' He blushed as he asked. Masters realized with a shock that table wines had not occurred to him. Mentally he gave Hill full marks.

'We didn't have wine, Sergeant, because Cora Dent said Sally couldn't have any, and as a good hostess she didn't want one guest to feel out of it. In any case, too much wine is drunk with meals. It makes you feel too full, so I didn't mind, and I don't suppose the men did.'

The alderman agreed that he'd not missed the wine. He'd made up for it later with Harry Dent's brandy in any case.

'A liqueur seemes to be a funny sort of drink for a diabetic to take,' Hill continued.

'Only one drink a week, Sergeant. And a very little one at that.'

'But it's very syrupy and sweet. According to the books they're not forbidden, but they're not good.'

Mrs Bancroft said simply, 'Sally liked liqueurs.'

'You're sure Mr Dent did give her a little one when he poured out?' asked Masters. 'He didn't try to be over-generous—because he's a generous host or because he was out to play a joke or anything like that?'

'Nothing like that. Mr Dent poured the brandy for the men, but Mrs Dent poured the women's drinks. She was always very careful to see that Sally got no more than was good for her. And I think that answers the sergeant's question, too.'

Masters lit his pipe. 'Well, that seems to dispose of the meal. Was there anything at all about the evening that struck you as out of the ordinary? Any remark, any action, any coming and going that struck you as odd?'

'Perfectly ordinary evening as far as I can recall,' Bancroft said. 'Just general chatter. Nothing very serious. Nothing very remarkable. That's what makes it seem so improbable as a prelude to murder. Are you absolutely sure there was foul play? I mean, a girl in her condition is very likely to fall into a coma, I understand, and if there was nobody with her to help . . .'

'Medical opinion is that her coma was too rapid to be natural and its seriousness too great to be normal. And her insulin was found to be useless,' Masters explained.

'Quite. Then why are you so interested in what she had to eat?'

'I like to cover every possibility, Mr Bancroft. As a point of fact, what I am doing by questioning you about the food is eliminating it from the list of causes. When I've eliminated what I can, what's left must contain the truth.'

'Of course. Stupid of me, one forgets that elimination is as important as elucidation, and that the one complements the other.'

'What are you going on about, Kenneth? Mr Masters asked if we'd noticed any odd comings and goings.'

'I know. I was telling him we didn't.'

'Not at the Dent house. But when he said comings and goings he reminded me.'

'What of?'

'When we were going there on Saturday night. Do you remember? The girl we saw.'

'Of course. The handsome one that young Brian used to knock about with at one time. I always liked the look of her. Cora didn't care for her, though. What was her name?'

'Clara Breese.'

'That's it. I ought to have remembered. I met her at that Friends of the Hospital affair.'

Masters noted that Hill stiffened visibly in his chair at the mention of Clara Breese. He himself felt a surge of excitement. Something? Or nothing? He would have to find out. Clara Breese somewhere near the Dent house at seven or thereabouts on Saturday evening. She hadn't mentioned that to Green. He could imagine Green's reaction when he heard about it. Particularly as he'd taken something of a shine to Miss Breese. 'What affair was this?' he asked Bancroft.

'I'm chairman of the Hospital Friends. An organization which devotes its energies to bettering the conditions in local hospitals. We achieve quite a bit, but we're chiefly concerned in raising money. Garden fêtes, coffee mornings, raffles. You know the sort of thing. Everybody who has used the hospital in the past year is asked to sell a book of raffle tickets. We collect a fair amount that way. But when it comes to spending the money, the fighting starts. One wants this and one wants that. Committees!'

'It's not quite as bad as that, but Ken's right,' Cordelia added. 'We collect the money amicably and then squabble over how to spend it. Ken had a good idea when he took over the chair. He formed an advisory committee of specialists. That's where people like Cora Dent came in. Being a dietitian, she could see what the food in hospital was like, and although we could do little to change it, we could use her recommendations as a basis for buying simple extras. Then there are the library trolleys and kiddies toys and so on. We got teachers and people like that to help and do the buying. It has worked quite well.'

'Where does Clara Breese fit into this?'

'Clara? It was when we decided to buy new curtains for the wards and redecorate some of them. Brian and Clara were friendly at the time, so Cora Dent brought in Clara to design and choose materials. That's when Kenneth met her. Clara made little models to show off her suggestions to the committee. Very good they were, too. Just made out of cardboard but cleverly done.'

'So you saw Clara on Saturday night?' Masters asked.

'Yes. I wondered what she was doing near the Dents. It's well over a year since I've seen her.'

'About seven o'clock?'

'A bit after. Perhaps ten past.'

'She was visiting an aunt in Gloucester last Saturday. Perhaps the aunt lives near the Dents,' Masters suggested.

'She has an aunt near there, has she? Oh, then that explains it. She was walking towards us, you know, as we were going.'

'That means she was walking away from the Dents' house?'

'Towards the city.'

'Well, that's one little coming and going. Any more?'

Cordelia shook her head. Kenneth said, 'I don't see where Clara Breese comes into this. Just because she was visiting relatives in Gloucester.'

'There's no suggestion that she is implicated in any way, sir,' replied Masters. 'But she happens to have been one of Miss Bowker's partners and a one-time friend of her fiancé. It will do her no harm to be eliminated as a possible suspect, will it?'

'I suppose not.'

'By the way, perhaps you could tell me. What's the pub Mr Dent goes to for his Sunday lunchtime drink? I was told that he and Brian went out for a lunchtime drink, but I was too busy at the time to make a mental note of the place.'

Bancroft got hastily to his feet. 'I'm sorry. I'm forgetting my duties. Let me get you a drink.'

'No. Please, no. That wasn't a hint. I'm due for a pint afterwards . . .'

'With Harry Dent? Well, it's not a pub he goes to.'

'No? I could have sworn . . .'

'Club. The Tontine.'

'Not a name you hear every day,' Cordelia said. 'And quite silly really. So easy to forget. And quite meaningless in this case. The last survivor takes all, indeed! They sign up new members every year.'

'You've got it wrong, Coddy,' her husband said. 'When the club was started, the people who put up the money agreed to receive no dividends nor expect the return of their money for a fixed period of—I think—about five years. And that's a form of tontine, too. That's where the name came from.'

'Really? And I'd always imagined them waiting for each other to die.'

'Well, I'll be getting along,' Masters said. 'Thank you for the talk and the information.'

'Are you going to the Tontine?' Bancroft asked.

'Not straight away. There are four of us. I've got to pick up the other two.'

'I see. I was going to say I'd take you.'

'Thank you, but there's no need to drag you out.'

'I'm a member.'

'But you weren't going today, were you?'

'No.'

'That's what I thought. Thanks all the same. We'll find our way there quite easily.'

When they were in the car, Hill said, 'You definitely gave him the impression Dent had invited you to this club.'

'I was careful not to say that Dent had invited me.'

'Then how did you know about it?'

'Brian Dent told me he and his father went out for their usual drink at Saturday lunchtime. It seemed likely that what was "usual" might include Sunday as well as Saturday. And men in their position usually have either a favourite pub or a club they get into the habit of going to at certain times.'

'So we're going to this Tontine place?'

'Not yet. We could have gone straight there if it had been a pub. But a club's for members only—and their guests.'

'So we've got to find somebody to take us?'

'That's right.'

'Then why didn't you accept Bancroft's offer?'

'Because I didn't want him bowling up to Dent and saying, "I've brought your guests." Dent hasn't invited us.

I want it to appear a casual meeting, otherwise I could call on Dent in his office tomorrow.'

Hill thought about this for a moment. Then: 'What now?'

'Stop at the first phone box. I want to call the Chief Super.'

'The Tontine?' Hook said. 'I'm a member myself, but I don't often go. Not at lunchtimes. I never drink in the middle of the day because I never know when I might be called out to . . .'

'Break your rules today. In honour of your guests from Scotland Yard. It's important, sir.'

After a few moments, Hook agreed. When they got back into the car, Masters said, 'I want a specimen envelope.'

Hill took from his pocket one of the plain white envelopes he carried for holding small material clues. Masters thanked him, took out his tin of Warlock Flake and carefully emptied the unrubbed tobacco into the envelope. He put the envelope into the glove compartment of the car, and the empty tin into his pocket. Hill watched with amazement which grew into incredulity when Masters tapped out a perfectly good fill, only half smoked, from his pipe. Masters looked up and grinned. 'Stage props,' he said. 'Right, Sergeant, drive on. The Chief Super's house. He's expecting us.'

An hour and a half later, Masters and Hill returned to the Bristol. Green and Brant had almost finished lunch. 'We waited long enough for you,' Green said.

'Sorry we're late,' answered Masters. 'We've been tanking up.'

'That's what I thought.'

Masters said no more. Hill took his cue from Masters

and didn't mention the visit to the Tontine. 'How's the alderman?' Green asked.

'Blooming. He's got a nice wife. The sort I think you would like.'

'Just my luck. We're bashing around here without a clue and when the only decent woman in the case is interviewed I'm not among those present.'

'What about Clara Breese? You told me she was all right.'

'Quite a nice bit of frippet. But too young for me. I like a mature woman.'

'Well, I don't know whether you'll get to meet Cordelia Bancroft, but you'll definitely have to see young Clara again—tonight, after she's finished the day's window-dressing.'

Green brushed biscuit crumbs from the table with his right hand, caught them in his left, and trickled them on to his plate. 'That's the worst of cream crackers. They fluther about so much.' He looked across at Masters who was tackling tongue and Russian salad. 'Beetroot's another think I don't like. It makes everything too bloody. What's this about Clara Breese?'

'She was seen by the Bancrofts at ten past seven last Saturday night quite near the Dents' place,' Hill said.

Green flung his napkin on to the table. 'Hell. So she bamboozled me.'

'Told you only half the truth, I suspect,' Masters commented.

'I'd like to dust her transparent pantie linings for her.'

'Who wouldn't?' Brant asked.

'Where does Breese's aunt live?' Masters inquired.

'Cambridge Road.'

'Where's that?'

'In the same direction from here as the Dents'. Remember when I took you out there we stopped at lights before turning left?'

'Yes.'

'If we'd gone straight on for a hundred yards and then turned left we'd have come to Cambridge Road. I'd say at a guess that aunty's house is a quarter of a mile from the Dents'.'

'It doesn't mean Breese was actually at the Dents',' Green said.

'Perhaps she didn't actually call there—or even go near,' replied Masters. 'But let's suggest to her that she did.'

'Why? What good will that do?'

'You said she's moping over Brian Dent.'

'So?'

'She came all the way from Cheltenham to see an aunt who isn't in, but who lives practically next door. Wouldn't a girl in her state—just for old times' sake—be tempted to walk that way?'

'I can't see it.'

'I can,' Hill broke in. 'If she's as natty a bit of stuff as you say she is, I can't see her being alone on a lovely Saturday afternoon and evening for nothing. So she wanted to see her aunt. O.K. But the aunt was out. I'd expect a girl like her to hop the next bus home and date some boy friend for the rest of the day. But what does Clara do? She moons about. Going to the cathedral and pictures alone? No!'

'You don't believe her?' Green asked.

'She lied, didn't she?'

Green snorted in disgust.

Masters said, 'I believe she went where she said. But a girl who finds herself at a loose end practically on the doorstep of the man she's still got a yen for would find her feet taking her that way willy-nilly.'

'To do what?'

'Nothing, I expect. Just look. And that would put her in the mood to take herself off to the pictures alone instead of rushing home to arrange an alternative late date.'

Green was unconvinced. 'Where does it get us if she did walk past the house?'

'It helps to keep the pot boiling,' Masters said. 'Makes us appear omniscient . . .'

'Om what?'

'Makes us look as if we knew more than we do.' Masters helped himself to Brie and breakfast biscuits.

'Now I know we're out of our depth,' Green said. 'We're having to start something to see what happens.'

'What's wrong with that?' asked Brant. 'It's a recognized technique.'

'It's a policy of despair.'

'I'm not despairing,' Masters answered. 'As I told you, I'm confident. Now, what about Heatherington-Blowers? Any word from him?'

'Nothing.' Green said. 'I reckon he's another of 'em.'

'What?'

'Bum steers.'

'Why?'

'He hasn't sparked yet, has he? Probably gone home for lunch and fallen asleep after it. And that's what we'd do if we had any nous.'

To Green's surprise Masters said, 'Good idea. We're at a standstill until we hear from Heatherington-Blowers, and until we can call on Breese. We'll meet for tea about a quarter past four unless something crops up in the meanwhile.'

'What are you going to do, Chief?' asked Hill.

'I'm going for a walk.'

'In this heat?'

'You're not going for a walk with no object in mind,' Green accused him.

'No. I want to take a look at the windows Sally Bowker dressed. The ones the Chief Super mentioned. And I might also visit the cathedral.'

Hill asked, 'Do you mind if I come with you?'

7

When they met at teatime, Green asked, 'Well? Any more bright ideas? Has Heatherington-Blowers called?'

'Don't get impatient,' said Masters. 'Have a crab sandwich instead.'

Green took two, lifted the top layer off one of them to examine the contents, saying, 'I never trust paste sandwiches.'

The lounge at the Bristol was fairly full. Masters had no desire to discuss his case within earshot of fellow guests, so he devoted himself to having tea. Green misread his intentions and regarded his avoidance of any mention of the case as another indication that the investigation was not progressing. Masters guessed this. Got a certain amount of pleasure out of the situation. He'd not tried to mislead Green. Had done the opposite, in fact, by stressing that he had gone a long way towards solving the problem. But Green, mistrustful by nature, had not believed him. Masters decided to let him stew in his own juice. Certainly it was an unusual case. As odd as Dick's hatband. But that was no reason for Green to be vociferously disbelieving.

Green, for his part, was mentally accusing Masters of being little short of a mountebank. Pretending the case was all over bar the shouting when as far as he could see there was no shred of proof to indicate the guilt of anybody concerned with Sally Bowker.

He felt the usual dislike of Masters rise in his gorge. Noted the slim hands as Masters stirred a cup of tea. Decorative but useless in Green's opinion. An anomaly. Almost a deformity in so big a man. Now, it appeared, he was looking at Clara Breese to help him out of the corner his boasting had forced him into. Green reflected that it would be just Masters' luck for something to turn up from that direction. Just as it was his own luck that he, when interviewing Clara Breese, had failed to ferret out anything useful. On the whole, Green felt slightly fed up with life in general, and with Chief bloody Inspector Masters in particular.

Hill was officiating at the tea pot. Green said sourly, 'Teem me a cup more bellywash.'

'It's not that bad.'

'It's a matter of opinion. They're using tea bags, not the proper stuff.'

'It's the same tea whether it's in bags or loose,' Brant said.

'You mind your own barrow. If you can't push it, shove it. I was talking to Sarn't Hill.'

'Sorry.'

Masters eased his chair away from the table. 'I'll be back, so don't squeeze the pot. I think I'd better call Heatherington-Blowers.'

Green hoped Masters would get a flea in his ear. He was disappointed. Inside five minutes Masters was back. 'They're being thorough. They're still at it,' he said.

'Doing what?'

'Bruce, the bacteriologist, is evidently a methodical man. He's going through the table of elements one by one, from A to Z, testing for traces.'

'How far's he got?' asked Green.

'About two-thirds of the way.'

'How many's that?'

'About seventy-five, I think. I believe there are something like a hundred elements these days. The list has grown a bit these last few years.'

'I thought there were only four—earth, water, air and fire,' Green said.

'Quite right. I was talking about chemical elements.'

Green grunted and lit a Kensitas.

'We won't get an answer before nine tonight. At least that's Bruce's estimate. So I suggest we go to Cheltenham to see Clara Breese, and hope that by the time we get there she'll have finished her day's work.'

She was wearing jeans. Cherry-picker red ones that clung round her seat and upper thighs and hugged her calves like jodhpurs. Above them she had a white shirt with the sleeves rolled up above the elbow, showing brown arms and strong wrists. Privately Masters thought she looked like a proud, young goddess. The appearance of Green and himself at the door didn't appear to disconcert her. 'The second instalment of the inquisition?' she asked. 'Come up. We might as well be comfortable.'

Masters could see the muscles of her buttocks and thighs rippling under the tight, thin material as she went up the stairs before him. He was reminded of an athlete—strength, power and co-ordination.

When they reached the sitting-room, Green said, 'Miss Bracegirdle not home yet?'

'She's been and gone. A date with a long-haired musician,' Clara said off-handedly.

Masters accepted her offer of a chair and then said, 'Miss Breese, you didn't tell Inspector Green the whole truth about your activities last Saturday. Why?'

'You mean I lied? I didn't, you know.'

'I said the whole truth. Why didn't you tell him you had been out a second time to your aunt's house, and had been wandering round the area in the early evening?'

'Because I didn't think he'd be interested in the name of every street I went down, nor in the number of the bus I caught, or the colour of the conductor's eyes.'

'Quite right, Miss Breese. But your wanderings took you pretty close to the Dent house. And we are interested in that, as you well know.'

'What the hell!' It was a listless retort. 'I didn't know I was going that way. You won't believe me, I dare say, but I just walked.'

'I'll believe you, Miss Breese—if you tell me exactly what you did, who you saw and so forth, to make it a convincing tale.'

'That's just the point. I can't. I called a second time at my aunt's house. After all, that's what I went to Gloucester for. She still wasn't at home. Then I literally wandered away. I didn't even know I was going towards the Dents'. I didn't notice anybody or anything. I was in a dream. My feet just took me there.'

'So you saw nobody?'

'No.'

'You got right up to the Dents' front gate?'

Clara sat up. 'No. I didn't. I didn't go that far.'

'How d'you know, if you were in a dream?'

She sank back again. 'I came to, just in time.'

'What woke you up?'

'A woman, coming out of the gate.'

'Dents' gate?'

'Yes.'

'You were close enough to see her?'

She nodded. 'I was on the other side of the road, and this woman came out. I noticed her and suddenly realized where I was.'

'Did you know the woman?'

'No.'

'A friend of Mrs Dent, perhaps?'

'I should think not. This one looked like a new maid—I mean one taken on since I was last there.'

'They had a maid in those days?'

'No. A gaggle of chars in the mornings, I think.'

'What did this woman look like?'

'Nothing on earth. Gingery. You know, that pale ginger

hair that has no body to it and goes all wispy. With a thin pale face, freckles, and no eyebrows to be seen. She looked damn bad-tempered, I can tell you that.'

'She appeared to be in a bad mood at the time?'

'Oh, no. I meant generally. She looked as if she'd got a slice of lemon in her mouth.'

'What was her figure like? Her size?'

'She was a neat sort of body, I suppose. Not very big. Taller than Win, but not gargantuan like me.'

'You do yourself an injustice, Miss Breese.'

She smiled for the first time. 'That's because you're no stumpy yourself. We belong to the same club.'

'No. Ask Inspector Green.'

'I shouldn't lose any sleep over my figure if I were you, Miss,' Green said. 'I know what men like, and you've got it all right—but a bit more than most, that's all.'

'Thank you.'

Green went on: 'But it doesn't mean we're very happy about you. You should have told me . . .'

'I couldn't. I've been in a gloom for months now. I just couldn't.'

'We understand,' Masters said. 'Now did you see anybody else near the Dent house other than the maid?'

'No. And I'm not saying it was the maid. You know, I've never given her a thought since the moment I saw her, but since you've been here, talking about her, I've began to feel that I might have seen her somewhere else, before. But I can't think when or where.'

'Try the hospital in Gloucester,' Masters suggested. 'When you went there to design the curtains and decorations.'

She stared at him for a moment and then said slowly, 'Yes. That's it. In a nurse's uniform. Her hair was under a cap then. That's what fooled me. But now you mention it I can remember the no-eyebrows effect at a few paces.

You're very clever, aren't you! And how did you get to know about the hospital curtains? You haven't been talking to Brian about me, have you?'

Masters smiled. 'Of course not. We're not so dim. Alderman and Mrs Bancroft told me how well you'd treated them.'

'I see. Would you like a drink? Cyprus sherry or vin rosé's all we've got.'

'Sherry, please. I'm not a great wine drinker.'

'You can refuse if you want to.'

'I'll do that only if the bottle's empty.'

She turned to Green. He said, 'Me, too. I *like* Cyprus sherry. I buy it myself. I don't know enough about it to buy the dear stuff.'

'You're both gorgeous men. Thank God for a bit of sanity and understanding.'

As she handed him his glass, Green said, surprisingly, 'Thanks. You'll feel better now, you know.'

'I feel better already. Cheers!'

It was ten past nine when Heatherington-Blowers finally rang. Masters was called to the phone from the garden where the four of them were sitting to get what cool the still-bright evening offered.

'Ah! Masters,' Heatherington-Blowers said. 'I think we'd better meet rather than gas on this thing.'

'Right, sir. Where and when?'

'What about the pub you're in? Both Bruce and I could do with a drink.'

'We're in the garden at the moment. I can organize a private room if you like.'

'The garden sounds wonderful after being cooped up all day in this shed of a laboratory. Ten minutes suit you?'

'Fine, sir. I'll line them up ready. Beer or whisky?'

'Beer for both of us—at any rate to begin with.'

Hill and Brant moved away at Green's suggestion to leave room at the table for the two newcomers. When they came—met by Masters at the front door of the Bristol—Hill, keeping his eyes open, collected the tankards of Worthington.

Heatherington-Blowers was dressed in old grey slacks and a cream bush jacket. He was, Masters judged, about fifty-five, very bald, with a sunburned pate fringed with grey hair. Little broken veins dotted his cheeks and nose end. He was a fair-sized man, running to girth through age rather than any other reason. Bruce looked like a be-spectacled schoolmaster. Pale, thin face, heavy-lensed glasses, a hooky nose and dark hair. He wore a brown suit, and carried a large book tucked into his shoulder, like a parson carrying his Bible into the pulpit to deliver a sermon.

Masters led them through to the garden and introduced them to Green. They sat at the table. Heatherington-Blowers drank deep. Bruce sipped.

Heatherington-Blowers said, 'I've been cursing you for many hours, Masters. You and your bright ideas! But you were right. Zinc. And you'll kindly note that zed comes right at the end of the alphabet.'

Masters said, dazedly, 'Zinc?'

'Very interesting indeed,' said Bruce. 'Of course it would have helped had we known what we were looking for. As it was we only succeeded by carrying out a most exhaustive process of elimination. Even so, I had begun to despair by the time we got to the last letter of the alphabet. And your floorcloth wasn't the ideal source of material, you know. Very sparse. Very sparse indeed.'

'Somebody had rinsed it,' Heatherington-Blowers said accusingly.

Masters said apologetically, 'The dead girl. Not us. We preserved it just as we found it.'

'Ah, well. You've justified your request for forensic help. Now what?'

'Zinc. What about it?'

'Oh, yes. Bruce has brought along *Martindale* for reference.' Bruce opened the book at a marked page. Heatherington-Blowers went on: 'You must realize, that tests such as we've carried out today, leaching the material to be tested out of an old floorcloth, give us no opportunity for telling you how much zinc there was in the body.'

'You would need the various organs for that?'

'No. Useless, I'm pleased to say. It lets me off the hook for not finding it at the post-mortem. Zinc sulphate—which is what it was—is eliminated in the vomit. That means I could only have made an estimate if I'd been given a proper sample of vomit. But we are able to say from today's tests that there was zinc sulphate present, and a significant amount of it. Which there certainly shouldn't have been. And as zinc sulphate is an emetic, it is logical to suppose that emesis was produced by its presence in the body. That was what you asked us to discover. We've done our part. How it got there is for you to find out.'

'Thank you,' Masters said.

'It's not an emetic that's used today,' Bruce said. 'I've never known it used myself, but I'll leave you *Martindale*. You'll get the information from there. Let me have it back tomorrow, won't you?'

'Without fail.'

'You can collect our written report at the same time.'

'How about another?' asked Green.

'Rather. It wasn't the sort of day to spend in a stuffy laboratory, handling a vomit rag. I need good clean beer to wash the taste away.'

'Hear, hear,' Heatherington-Blowers said.

While Green was away Masters said, 'I don't know how to thank you, gentlemen . . .'

'By shutting up about it and allowing us to enjoy a decent drink at your expense,' said Heatherington-Blowers. 'By jove it's nice out here. I'll remember this as a place to come to. Hello! The sun's not quite down yet, but we've got the fairy lights on. Jolly nice. You can see right into the pub and the bars.'

'In lovely weather there's no better place than a good, old British pub,' Bruce said. 'I feel better already. And here comes our beer.'

At breakfast-time the next morning, Green said, 'You shied off to bed like a long dog last night. Never a word about how the situation is affected by the saw-bones finding zinc sulphate among the puke.'

'Because there was nothing more I could tell you without doing a bit of study first,' Masters replied.

'We could have discussed it.'

'Without knowing exactly what we were talking about? It would have been a waste of time, and you know it. As it was, I didn't, as you suggest, get to bed for some hours.'

Green grunted and tackled a bowl of breakfast cereal which had been growing more and more soggy as he talked. He sucked the milk out of each spoonful before starting to chew. Both the noise and the sight irritated Masters. While he waited for his boiled eggs he half turned from the table and opened his *Daily Telegraph*.

Brant and Hill came down together. 'Might as well stoke up this morning,' the latter said. 'There'll be plenty doing today.'

It was a question in the form of a statement. Intended to lure Masters out. It succeeded. He said, 'I shall want to know where that zinc sulphate came from, and who bought it.'

'That means a round of the chemists.'

Masters nodded, and folded his paper small as the eggs

135

were placed in front of him. 'And also, I want you to go to the hospital to return *Martindale* and collect the written report from Bruce. While you're there, ask the chief pharmacist if he or any of his staff have noticed any unauthorized person snooping round any of the pharmacopoeias recently.'

'What sort of person?'

'Any sort. Young, old, male, female, staff or outsider.'

Hill didn't reply. Masters obviously wasn't in the mood for idle back-chat. It made social contact sticky, but he knew from experience it was a good sign as far as the case was concerned. Masters always grew taciturn near the end. Hill often wondered why. Any other man would be cheerful, overtly proud of his achievement. Not that Masters wasn't proud of his. He was. Proud as a peacock and twice as vain. But not at this stage. Later, when all was signed, sealed and delivered. Then he would expect acclaim—and get it.

'And what about me?' Green asked.

'Would you like to tackle Nurse Ward?'

'She's in it, too?' Brant inquired.

'Up to the neck,' Green said. He turned to Masters. 'What about you?'

'I'll be with you, but I'll tackle Dr Sisson—separately. As each one completes, report to the Police Station. I should be with Hook by then.'

Green started on bacon and eggs. 'You know,' he said, 'I really believed we'd be out of our depth over this case, but here we are, home and in the dry.'

'Are we?' Brant asked. 'I haven't the slightest idea who killed her. Or why. Have you?'

Green said airily, 'Not the actual person, no. But we've got all the facts. They only need sorting, and the picture should be as clear as day.'

Masters said, 'I mentioned yesterday that I was short on

proof. Finding zinc sulphate on that rag only confirms a theory I formed. I made a mistake about ipecacuanha, but the theory was, nevertheless, basically sound. Your work today will confirm whether my theory about the identity of the murderer was correct or whether I've made a mistake in that, too. For that reason I'll not give you my ideas—in case they prejudice your investigations.'

Hook was not in his office when Masters arrived at the Station. The sergeant on duty said, 'He went off for his walk at twelve, sir. He'll take an hour over it, then go home to lunch, and be back here about two.'

Masters cursed his luck. He had been obliged to wait until the end of surgery before seeing Sisson. Monday surgeries, as Sisson had explained, are noticeably larger than those on any other day of the week. After that, the talk with the doctor had lasted longer than Masters had intended. It had been a difficult time. No doctor will readily believe that his own ancillary staff can be implicated in the murder of patients. Sisson was no exception. Then there had been the technical questions. Sisson had taken his time, doing a thorough job. By the time Masters had been able to leave the surgery, the morning had gone, and Sisson's visits were a long way behind schedule.

And now Hook was out beating the bounds.

Masters said to the desk sergeant, 'I'm expecting the other members of my team to report here. Please ask them to come on to the Bristol. We'll all be back here at two.'

'I'll see to it, sir. And I'll let the Chief Superintendent know you're coming, if I see him before you do.'

'Thanks.'

Masters had hardly reached the hotel, on foot, than Hill and Brant, who were using the car, arrived too. They joined him in the bar. He noticed immediately that they were far from jubilant.

'What luck?'

'None,' Hill said. 'We've been to every chemist. Most of them don't stock zinc sulphate—except in made-up ointments—and the others say they haven't sold any for years except to a few kids with chemistry sets.'

Brant added, 'And the hospital pharmacist says he's seen nobody nosing round his books and in any case visitors are not allowed in the dispensary. So if anybody had been in, they wouldn't say.'

Masters thought for a moment. 'Chemistry sets, you said?'

Hill nodded.

'Right. Off you go. Toy shops, model supply shops—anywhere likely to sell chemistry equipment and substances to children.'

'Now, Chief?'

'Yes. Now. And while you're at it, call on the librarian at the public library. Ask him if he's noticed anybody in the reference room looking at pharmacopoeias lately.'

The two sergeants left, slightly put out that they hadn't been allowed to have just one drink, and faced with the prospect of missing lunch.

When Green joined him, Masters suggested they should take their drinks out into the privacy of the garden. There Green reported at length. Masters, satisfied with what he heard, suggested lunch, so that they could be at the station by two o'clock. They were eating when Hill and Brant returned, this time looking decidedly more cheerful.

'So you reckon you know who killed my little Sally?' Hook asked.

Masters, puffing unconcernedly at his pipe, said, 'Yes. I know.'

'Who?'

'Cora Dent.'

Hook looked more than surprised. He stared in disbelief. After a few seconds he said, 'I don't believe it.'

'Why not?'

'Because ... well, because she's a respected and respectable woman.'

'You mean she's the wife of a rich man and friendly with all the leading lights?' asked Green.

Hook frowned. He ignored Green. 'I'll want some convincing before I make an arrest,' he said.

'Of course,' Masters answered. 'We're here to give you the facts. How you proceed after that is entirely your affair. It's your case.'

'And I wish it wasn't.'

'I know.'

'I've been troubled ever since I took you to the Tontine yesterday lunchtime. The way you pulled that fast one on Harry Dent.'

'Fast one?'

'Oh, I noticed it. I didn't know what you were getting at, but I knew you were up to something. You had to be, otherwise you wouldn't have asked me to take you there.'

'I wanted some information. I believe that if I'd asked a direct question I'd not have got a true answer. So I resorted to a little ruse. Nothing more.'

'What happened?' Green asked.

'We got to the Tontine,' the Chief Superintendent replied, 'and saw Harry and Brian Dent having a drink. We went over and joined them as they were obviously the only people—other than myself—who knew the Chief Inspector.'

'That was the object of the exercise, sir,' Hill said.

'I know that. Young Brian left us after a bit to chat with somebody else. As soon as he'd gone, the Chief here pulls out a tobacco tin, opens it, and says, "Oh dear, it's empty, and I don't suppose they sell my brand here." Harry Dent says, "No, they don't. I've never even heard of it." Then the Chief says, "I could have sworn there was quite a lot in it first off this morning." Dent says, "That's always happening." Chief says, "Like your liqueurs, eh? You thought they were full and they weren't." Dent says, "Something of the sort." Chief says, "But this is worse. I'm certain my tin had a few leaves left only half an hour ago." Dent says, "Like my liqueurs again. I can swear that when I went to the cupboard on Thursday to check up on the gin and whisky there was half a bottle each of Drambuie and Benedictine. But I was wrong. And the girls had to do with Anisette, just like you'll have to do with one of my cigarettes, or go without a smoke." '

Hill grinned. 'What's wrong with that?' Green asked.

'Nothing. Except as soon as we got in the car outside the club the Chief had mysteriously found enough tobacco for another fill. I know I'm not a D.C.S., but I can see a right mountain of hokum when it suddenly appears in front of me.'

'If you are unhappy about that little ruse, sir,' Masters asked, 'would you prefer me to make my report to the Chief Constable in writing?'

Hook lit a cigarette. 'No I wouldn't, and you know it. But that's not what I call good police work.'

'Maybe not, sir, but I could think of no other way of getting to know whether the liqueur bottles had been full or empty that week, and I had to know without suggesting to Dent that I was suspicious of either his wife or son. And I assure you it was the only ruse I used during the investigation.'

'I'll take your word for it. Now what about the rest of the proof?'

'When we arrived, we knew nothing about diabetes and diabetic comas. Dr Sisson, however, very kindly gave us a lesson on it, and one of the points which he stressed was that the coma brought about by lack of insulin takes a long time to come on, naturally. Up to forty-eight hours. Sally Bowker, according to Sisson, must have been in a coma by soon after midnight on Saturday, and she died less than twenty-four hours later.

'Now her coma must have come upon her inexplicably quickly. She was fit when she underwent a medical examination in the morning, she was fit in the afternoon when she was out viewing a house, and she was fit in the early evening when she went swimming. And she felt well enough to eat a good supper and drink a liqueur. Yet by midnight she was too far gone to summon help. This could mean only one thing—that her condition had been induced in some way.

'When we visited Miss Bowker's flat, we noticed that the bathroom, with its door shut for several days in this hot weather, smelt not only of stale air, as one would expect, but of vomit. This suggested the girl had been sick, and to support the suggestion, we found a floor rag which smelt as though it had been used for mopping up vomit and only imperfectly rinsed afterwards.

'Dr Sisson told us that violent sickness which robbed the body of its essential minerals and all its fluid content was a significant factor in bringing on diabetic coma which, in turn, if not expertly treated, would lead to death through collapse of the blood and respiratory systems.

'Dr Sisson also told us that Sally Bowker had been taught what the first signs of diabetic coma were, and how to combat them. The fact that she gave herself an additional shot of insulin proves that she took the precautions she had been taught.

'Why, then, were the steps she took ineffective? We know the answer. Her insulin was useless.

'My immediate thought on hearing Dr Sisson say that

vomiting was a significant factor in bringing on diabetic coma was to suppose that the vomiting had been induced by the administration of an emetic. Unless this had been done, there would have been no need for Miss Bowker to inject more insulin that night, and a useless injection the next day would be unlikely to achieve its object, because Miss Bowker would be out and about where, had she collapsed, other people would have come to her aid.

'That is why I was so insistent that an emetic had been administered. And at this point I must say that I am indebted to Inspector Green for his suggestion that the insulin Miss Bowker injected just before supper was also useless. I had overlooked that point, but it makes the work of the murderer more complete and sure. For a girl to eat a large meal under the impression that she is protected by insulin when, in fact, her body has no insulin, is itself a danger to health and must have been a contributory factor to the severity of the sickness and the coma which brought on death.'

Hook gritted his teeth at the thought. He threw cigarettes to Green, Brant and Hill. When he had blown out the match he said in a hard voice, 'Go on.'

Masters did so. 'So I set out to look for an emetic and a way of administering it. The only emetics I knew were common salt and ipecacuanha. Because to disguise a dose of common salt large enough to produce emesis would be virtually impossible, I discarded it. I thought about ipecac a little more. It appeared that this, too, was unlikely on several counts—difficulty of obtaining it in sufficient strength unobtrusively, its exceedingly bitter taste in strong doses, and so on. But, as I say, I was initially more interested in finding the way in which an emetic could have been administered. So, for the moment, I no longer concerned myself with the substance itself, and concentrated on the means by which it had been given, without her knowledge, to Sally Bowker. I asked myself the question, "What does a cook use for disguising taste in food?" The immediate answer was curry powder which, I have always understood, was originally used to disguise the taste of meat or fish that, before the days of refrigeration, was not always as wholesome as it might have been—particularly in hot countries. Curry, as you know, is made of turmeric and bruised spices. As far as I could tell, no turmeric—ginger—had been used in the preparation of Sally's last meal. But what about spices? There were no cloves, mace, nutmeg, cinnamon, peppermint . . . but I continued to go through every one I could think of . . . lemon, pepper, coriander, aniseed . . . It was when I came to aniseed that I knew I had found the method. At the Dent house was a bottle of aniseed—in liqueur form. Anisette. The ideal means of disguising an emetic. And Sally had drunk Anisette after dinner on the Saturday night—although she preferred Benedictine—because Anisette was the only liqueur available. Drinking a liqueur once a week at the Dent house was her one regular indulgence. If I possibly could, I had to know whether the fact that only Anisette was available that night was brought about by accident or design. I believe it was by design. The ruse you complained of, sir, was used to get Harry Dent to say that he was surprised that the other liqueurs were finished, because he had, or so he thought, noted only two nights earlier that the bottles were half full.'

Hook grunted what Masters took to be a sound of approbation or forgiveness for his behaviour at the Tontine.

Masters went on: 'So I came to the conclusion that the reason for there being only the one liqueur was to disguise the administration of an emetic to Miss Bowker. I was, incidentally, careful to inquire whether anybody else present at the supper party had suffered any ill effects. Nobody had.

'The emetic used was proving a problem. But as you know, sir, through you I approached Heatherington-Blowers and, thereafter, Bruce the bacteriologist. They very kindly agreed to test the floorcloth as no samples of the vomit itself had been available. They did not know what they were looking for, but eventually they found significant traces of zinc sulphate, which is a stomach irritant, and by this means produces emesis. Heatherington-Blowers pointed out that though zinc sulphate is a stomach irritant, there were no lesions on the stomach linings when he carried out the post mortem. This allowed him to state categorically that the zinc had been administered only a short time before the girl was sick. Zinc is eliminated entirely in vomit and that is the reason it had been overlooked in the post-mortem—it was not there itself, nor were any of its effects apparent, on the membranes of the stomach. So I felt safe in assuming Miss Bowker had been given an emetic shortly before her death, disguised in Anisette.

'Mrs Dent served the three ladies with their liqueurs. It was a habit of hers always to serve Miss Bowker her liqueur under the pretext of making sure that she was given no more than was good for her.'

Hook said, 'It's hard to believe. She liked Sally. Everybody did. Even old Harry Dent did—though I suppose he was a bit worried about his son being tied to an invalid all his days.'

'Quite,' Masters said. 'Mr Dent would rather his son's wife wasn't diabetic. So would we all. But it doesn't mean to say we try to kill off diabetics, or even that we don't like them. I believe Harry Dent became very fond of Sally before she became diabetic, and his affection for her continued. But he had natural qualms about her state of health and the effect it would have on his son's life. He *didn't* want his son tied to an invalid, but as that was what was going to happen, I think he accepted it, and he looked on the girl as his daughter. With great affection.

'With Mrs Dent it was different.

'I'd like you to understand, sir, that for the next few moments I am giving you my deductions, based on what I've learned from various sources, including yourself. Brian Dent is an only child. The most unfortunate type of only child—the one with the over-possessive mother. He himself admits this. No girl had ever been good enough for Brian—until Sally Bowker came along. Brian says that he dropped Clara Breese in favour of Sally of his own free will. I doubt this. He may have thought he did, but I believe that if Mrs Dent had approved of Clara, she would not have allowed Brian to drop her. Clara is a girl of strong will, with a mind of her own. Not the sort to allow Mrs Dent to have everything all her own way. Additionally, she is a penniless artist: a girl who must work for her living. Not at all a suitable wife for Brian in Cora Dent's eyes. Sally Bowker was a cheerful, but more pliant child. More likely to fall in with Mrs Dent's ideas. And in her case, her work was just a pastime. She came from a well-to-do family—father a farmer in a big way and owner of a thriving light-engineering company. Just the girl to make Brian a smart, pretty wife and Mrs Dent a daughter-in-law who wouldn't be difficult to manage.

'I don't say that Brian and Sally were not in love with each other. I think they were, and I think they would have made each other very happy. But I believe the engagement was only allowed to go through because Mrs Dent approved and showed her approval by offering no objections.

'The wedding was arranged, and then Miss Bowker was diagnosed as diabetic. This, I believe, upset Mrs Dent's applecart. You, yourself, told me, sir, that the wedding had been postponed. Why, I wonder?'

'Because Sally was ill, of course.'

'No, sir. Miss Bowker was no more ill a fortnight ago when she was originally to have been married, than she would have been in September at the revised date. I believe the first date was cancelled at Mrs Dent's insistence. She hoped there would be no marriage. Miss Bowker had, as Dr Sisson put it, a metabolic defect. Mrs Dent would not want an imperfect wife for her son. She was determined they shouldn't marry. But apart from the fact that Brian loved the girl and intended to marry her, he was formally engaged to her, and to break the engagement could have meant a breach-of-promise action with undesirable publicity—because the grounds for breaking the engagement would be such as would arouse public sympathy for the diabetic girl.

'So a new date was fixed by Miss Bowker. There was no reason for further delay. I believe that when she named the day, Miss Bowker signed her own death warrant. Mrs Dent realized that to save her son from what, in her eyes, seemed a calamitous marriage, she would have to get rid of the girl. From that moment on she began to prepare her scheme, so that when the opportunity arose, she would be ready to put it into operation.

'She was clever. She had shown affection for the girl before diabetes was diagnosed. She had to continue to show the same affection afterwards, in order not to antagonize her son and to put her in a stronger position for cancelling the wedding altogether. If Brian was to be her unwitting tool in breaking the engagement, he must not suspect hostility on her part, or the ploy might fail. So apparently all were on the best of terms even to the point of Mrs Dent offering the girl a present of five hundred pounds which she, Mrs Dent, never intended should be given or used. Maybe she also thought that this offer would throw people like us off the scent should the girl's death ever be investigated.'

'How do you know that?'

'I don't know it, but Inspector Green will bear me out when I say she went all artificially coy when the gift was mentioned on Saturday night. "Oh, Brian shouldn't have told you. It was just a little family secret." You know the attitude, sir. Sick-making.'

Hook nodded unhappily. 'You're a dab hand at drawing conclusions from attitudes that would escape the notice of other people.'

'I try to be, sir, because it helps. Particularly in cases like this. But to go on: Heatherington-Blowers and Bruce found a significant amount of zinc sulphate in the vomit. Sergeant Hill and Sergeant Brant visited all the local chemists to try to discover if anybody had bought zinc sulphate from them recently. No luck. But zinc sulphate is one of those fairly common chemicals that boys with chemistry sets mess about with. It is an odourless, colourless, efflorescent crystal or a white crystalline powder. Toy shops sell it in little cardboard drums to youngsters for experiments, because it's not poisonous. So we tried the toy shops. The proprietor of The Model Emporium remembers selling some a week or two ago to a middle-aged woman. Usually, boys buy it. That's why he can remember this well-dressed woman, with blue-rinsed hair, coming in for it. His description fits Mrs Dent. You will be asked to arrange an identity parade for him to make sure.'

Hook nodded.

'And also for one of the girl librarians. She remembers a woman coming to the reference department some weeks ago and asking to see the pharmacopoeias. This woman, too, had blue-rinsed hair, and the girl remembers seeing her about the town on various occasions, so identification should not be difficult.'

'Why should looking at pharmacopoeias be so important?' Hook asked.

'Because Mrs Dent, being a dietitian, would know the difficulties of disguising taste. She would know also—none better—the use of aniseed for this purpose. Hence the Anisette. But it would be better still to have an emetic with a less pronounced taste and no smell, if possible, even though it was to be given in Anisette.

'*Martindale*—the authority used by most doctors and chemists—lists seven emetics. Zinc sulphate is the last in the list, and according to the doctors I've spoken to, the least well known. In fact, some of them had never even heard of it as an emetic and, therefore, I am assuming that it was unknown to Mrs Dent, too, before she visited the library. I think I can satisfy you as to why she chose zinc sulphate. The seven emetics listed are antimony sodium tartrate, apomorphine, mustard flour, copper sulphate, ipecacuanha and other vegetable expectorants, sodium chloride, and finally zinc sulphate. As you know, two of them, mustard flour and sodium chloride—or common salt—are ordinary household condiments. But how would you disguise an emetic dose of ten grammes of mustard in a liqueur, or enough salt to do the trick in so small a drink? Impossible. That leaves five. But two of these, antimony sodium tartrate and apomorphine are injectables. So they were out, too. That leaves three. Our old friend ipecac—as everybody knows—is very bitter, and the amount needed to produce emesis is so large there would be no room left in a liqueur thimble for the Anisette, let alone enough to blanket the taste. Two left. Copper sulphate is blue. Everybody knows that. I think the thought of the colour steered her clear of copper sulphate, but I think it gave her the idea that these chemicals can be bought at places other than chemists' shops. She was left with zinc sulphate. And here the properties seemed very advantageous to her. An odourless white powder, very soluble in water—less than one part of water is needed to one part of zinc sulphate—with an emetic dose ranging from only six-tenths of a gramme up to two grammes maximum. In other words, an egg-spoonful of the liquid would be certain to do the trick. Admittedly there is an astringent, metallic taste, but not such that Anisette wouldn't cover it.

'I've already told you how easy zinc sulphate is to get hold of. What about its effects? Vomiting and incessant retching, followed by extreme prostration. Think of what happened to Sally Bowker. Exactly that. And to add to the suitability of zinc sulphate as a poison for a diabetic are these two facts—that it is eliminated from the body in the vomit as I've already explained; and that *Martindale* cites an example of a woman who, after swallowing one ounce of zinc sulphate became semi-comatose with—and note this bit particularly—a marked ketosis. She died despite insulin therapy.'

'What's that? Ketosis?'

'It's what diabetics get when their insulin is useless or they don't get enough of it. It's what brought on Sally Bowker's coma.'

Hook said bitterly, 'I see. It was all laid on very nicely for Cora Dent, wasn't it?'

'That's one way of putting it.' Masters paused for a moment to see if Hook had any further comment to make. As none came, he said, 'Shall we push on, sir?'

'Aye. But I'll order some tea first. I daresay you could do with giving your voice a rest.'

The tea came in. Masters appeared to be in a hurry. Before anybody had finished drinking he started talking again.

'I've told you how I believe Mrs Dent came to choose zinc sulphate as the emetic, and I think you can safely assume that she will be identified as having bought the chemical. Now we must turn to the insulin. You've all seen the aluminium carrying-case Miss Bowker used for her injection materials. A metal box with plastic compartments inside. Miss Bowker carried two bottles of insulin on this occasion—one with a single dose, the other full. The single dose she injected before supper, so we cannot state categorically that it was useless, but I believe it was, as Inspector Green suggested, and I hope you will see why I say so in a minute. We know the full bottle was useless. Tests proved it.

'Dr Sisson said the useless insulin was not toxic. That means that no poison had been added. Why then was it useless? The hint came when Brian Dent said Miss Bowker was careful never to leave her bag in the heat of the sun. Later, I read the instructions for keeping insulin. It must not be stored on a mantelpiece above a fire, in an airing-cupboard or anywhere too warm. An article on the manufacture of insulin says, and I quote: "Heat is enemy to insulin."

'Having established that, gentlemen, I had to look round for a source of heat. Quick heat, because Miss Bowker only left her bag in the downstairs cloakroom for the time she was swimming, and nobody could foresee how short a time that might be. In addition, I believe Mrs Dent—though prepared—only took the decision to act on that particular Saturday night at a quarter to seven the same evening. Why I say this will become clear later. But if you accept my word for it, you'll see that time was short. The meal was to be at seven thirty and Sally Bowker was meticulous in having her injection exactly half an hour before she ate a main meal. So Mrs Dent was pushed for time. At the most she could expect a quarter of an hour in which to work. At the least a minute or two. So, a slow gentle warmth would be no good for her purpose. The downstairs cloakroom is near the kitchen. In the kitchen was Mrs Dent, and Mrs Dent is the proud owner of an infra-red grill—also in the kitchen. I wandered along to the electricity showrooms yesterday afternoon. A model similar to Mrs Dent's was on display. Its loading is fifteen hundred watts, and it is advertised as being capable of cooking a steak to perfection in sixty seconds. If it will do that, how long will it take to render useless a phial of insulin to which an ordinary warm atmosphere is "enemy"? I suggest that Miss Bowker's carrying case was put bodily into the grill for a very short time. Thirty seconds, perhaps.'

'The whole box?' Green asked.

'I believe so. Otherwise the labels on the phials would have been singed. Sisson says there was no sign of that, but the plastic inside the box is slightly discoloured and misshapen. In my ignorance, when I first noted this, I thought it was staining and fair wear and tear. I was wrong. Insulin does not stain plastic. Another reason why I think the period was short was because the syringe was in a cylinder of industrial spirit. A prolonged period of fierce heat would have caused that to explode. It didn't do so. But what undoubtedly confirms my belief that the whole box was heated is the state of the reagent strips in their bottle. The impregnated portion of every strip is dark brown. When I first saw them, I naturally thought this was the correct colour. But whilst reading, I came across some information about them. They should be stored—like insulin—in a cool place. The impregnated portion, when in good condition, is white or cream: too much heat sends them brown, and in this state they are useless. I don't think that Sally Bowker, who was so careful about everything else, would carry useless testing strips. I believe they were submitted to greater than normal heat after she had packed them in her case.

'A very few seconds under the infra-red grill would render the insulin useless and the box could then be returned to Miss Bowker's handbag. When she came in a short time later she gave herself the first of the useless injections. Then she ate her meal, with her previous injection still carrying her over. Then she had the liqueur and emetic. Shortly afterwards she began to feel the effects. The meal had been taken at half-past seven. In less than three hours from the start of it, she was at home, feeling sick. Shortly after that she vomited, gave herself the second useless injection and then, I imagine, was seriously sick again and again, unable even to summon help. She made her way to her bed, lay down, prostrate, became comatose very quickly and then, much later, died.'

'It's too solid to be wrong,' Hook said. 'But how did Cora Dent know all that about an emetic and how to make insulin useless?'

Masters said, 'She made contact with Sisson's nurse, who in former days had been working in the diabetic clinic of the hospital. We heard from Miss Breese that Nurse Ward had visited Mrs Dent early on Saturday evening. She was seen leaving the house at a quarter to seven. I believe it was her report that decided Mrs Dent to act that night. You see, sir, Miss Bowker had told Dr Sisson only that morning that she and Brian intended to have children, and to start having them immediately they were married. Nurse Ward—with whom this particular conversation between Miss Bowker and Sisson was a very sore point—had obviously hurried to Mrs Dent to report it. For Mrs Dent this was the last straw. She was already prepared to murder Sally to prevent her marrying Brian; she was prepared to murder Sally immediately at the thought of her producing children which might, just possibly, but improbably, carry the same defect as their mother. A form of madness, no doubt. But to confirm what I say, Inspector Green will give us the gist of Nurse Ward's formal statement.'

'It's the old story,' Green said. 'Ward was flattered by the attention paid to her by Mrs Dent. It started soon after Bowker was diagnosed as diabetic. According to Ward, when she worked in the hospital, Mrs Dent, who was always in and out, never noticed her. Then I think Sally Bowker must have mentioned Nurse Ward at the Dents' house. There was an accidental meeting on purpose between Ward and Mrs Dent. Engineered by Dent in a coffee shop. Dent said, "You're Nurse Ward, aren't you? Yes, I thought I recognized you. My son's fiancée tells me you're looking after her now. Splendidly, she says. Do you mind if I have my coffee with you? Thank you. You must tell me all about diabetes so that I know how to look after Sally, too. Her parents are away, you know, and I feel so responsible for her." That was the form. As we know, Ward is keen on Sisson. Sisson was keen on Bowker, and Ward knew it. She would do anything to keep Bowker in cahoots with young Dent and away from Sisson. Ward and Mrs Dent met about once a month and, as Mrs Dent intended they should, the meetings deteriorated into little more than tittle-tattle sessions about Bowker. After each of Bowker's visits to the surgery, Ward reported what went on to Dent. Dent encouraged these meetings. Ward reported to her as usual on the Saturday that Bowker died—or, more correctly, the Saturday before she died.'

Green handed round the packet of Kensitas he had been holding while he spoke. He then went on: 'Nurse Ward admits she reported overhearing Miss Bowker tell Dr Sisson that she and young Dent intended to start a family immediately they were married.'

There was a short pause, then Masters continued: 'As I said a moment ago, I think that news infuriated Mrs Dent. Made her determined to act immediately. She saw Nurse Ward away at a quarter to seven—the visit hadn't been noticed by Dent, who was watching television, or by the youngsters, who were swimming—then she went into action. She first of all ruined the insulin. That would be the only tricky part, and it could only have taken her two or three minutes at the most—to open the bag, put the carrying-case under the heat, and then put it back in the bag.'

'It would be hot,' Green commented.

'They use tongs for these grills.'

'I know that. But putting it back in the bag.'

'Easy. The bag was in the cloakroom. Mrs Dent could carry in the hot case and lock the door behind her while she waited for the case to cool. If Miss Bowker had come along and tried the door, what would she think?'

'That Mrs D. was in there having a jimmy,' Green suggested.

'Quite. The natural assumption. So as soon as the case was cool enough, into the bag it could go. If Miss Bowker was waiting outside, flushing the lavatory would help convince her that Mrs Dent was in there for an innocuous purpose. After that, I expect, Mrs Dent made her solution of zinc sulphate—quite openly, because nobody would question her making a mixture in her own kitchen—carried it through to the wine cupboard, hid it there, took the Drambuie and Benedictine bottles, emptied them, and then took them back to the wine cupboard. Five minutes' work at most and, as I say, it wouldn't have mattered if anybody had seen her doing any of it except grilling the carrying-case and pouring away the liqueurs.

'The whole plan worked like clockwork. Nobody else could have been responsible. Brian was swimming until after Sally gave herself her first injection. Harry Dent didn't serve the Anisette. The Bancrofts didn't go into the kitchen or leave the table during the meal.'

Hook said heavily, 'And that's it?'

'Except for the identification parade and a check for Mrs Dent's fingerprints among those taken off Sally Bowker's bag. There are some of a woman other than Sally herself.'

'What about the carrying-case?'

'Too many of us handled that; and in any case, as they handle things with tongs or a fish slice in these infra-red grills there might not have been any identifiable ones. Anyhow, it's immaterial. You've got the whole story with material confirmation to support the circumstantial evidence.'

Hook got to his feet. 'I don't know how the devil you do it,' he said.

'My written report will be very much fuller. You'll find your answer in there.'

'Maybe. I doubt if even you can write up what you owe to commonsense and ability. However, that's not my affair. I'll have to arrest Cora Dent.'

'And we'll be going straight away if you don't mind, sir.'

'But I do mind. I've got Mr and Mrs Bowker coming over tonight. They'll want to thank you.'

Masters shivered mentally. 'Please tell them I had another urgent job waiting for me.'

'Is there really another one lined up already?' Hook said.

'I never knew the time when there wasn't,' replied Green.

On the road home, Green said, 'I didn't think you'd make it.'

'You mean you were dead scared we wouldn't.'

Green blustered. 'What d'you mean? Scared?'

'Because you're a sentimental old humbug. Right from the start you fell for that photo of Sally Bowker and you wanted to find her murderer so desperately you got scared that we shouldn't succeed.'

Green had the grace to blush.

THE PERENNIAL LIBRARY MYSTERY SERIES

Delano Ames

CORPSE DIPLOMATIQUE   P 637, $2.84
"Sprightly and intelligent."

> —*New York Herald Tribune Book Review*

FOR OLD CRIME'S SAKE   P 629, $2.84

MURDER, MAESTRO, PLEASE   P 630, $2.84
"If there is a more engaging couple in modern fiction than Jane and Dagobert Brown, we have not met them."
> —*Scotsman*

SHE SHALL HAVE MURDER   P 638, $2.84
"Combines the merit of both the English and American schools in the new mystery. It's as breezy as the best of the American ones, and has the sophistication and wit of any top-notch Britisher."
> —*New York Herald Tribune Book Review*

E. C. Bentley

TRENT'S LAST CASE   P 440, $2.50
"One of the three best detective stories ever written."
> —*Agatha Christie*

TRENT'S OWN CASE   P 516, $2.25
"I won't waste time saying that the plot is sound and the detection satisfying. Trent has not altered a scrap and reappears with all his old humor and charm."
> —*Dorothy L. Sayers*

Gavin Black

A DRAGON FOR CHRISTMAS   P 473, $1.95
"Potent excitement!"   —*New York Herald Tribune*

THE EYES AROUND ME   P 485, $1.95
"I stayed up until all hours last night reading *The Eyes Around Me*, which is something I do not do very often, but I was so intrigued by the ingeniousness of Mr. Black's plotting and the witty way in which he spins his mystery. I can only say that I enjoyed the book enormously."
> —*F. van Wyck Mason*

YOU WANT TO DIE, JOHNNY?   P 472, $1.95
"Gavin Black doesn't just develop a pressure plot in suspense, he adds uninfected wit, character, charm, and sharp knowledge of the Far East to make rereading as keen as the first race-through."   —*Book Week*

Nicholas Blake

THE CORPSE IN THE SNOWMAN P 427, $1.95
"If there is a distinction between the novel and the detective story (which we do not admit), then this book deserves a high place in both categories." —*The New York Times*

THE DREADFUL HOLLOW P 493, $1.95
"Pace unhurried, characters excellent, reasoning solid."
—*San Francisco Chronicle*

END OF CHAPTER P 397, $1.95
". . . admirably solid . . . an adroit formal detective puzzle backed up by firm characterization and a knowing picture of London publishing."
—*The New York Times*

HEAD OF A TRAVELER P 398, $2.25
"Another grade A detective story of the right old jigsaw persuasion."
—*New York Herald Tribune Book Review*

MINUTE FOR MURDER P 419, $1.95
"An outstanding mystery novel. Mr. Blake's writing is a delight in itself." —*The New York Times*

THE MORNING AFTER DEATH P 520, $1.95
"One of Blake's best." —Rex Warner

A PENKNIFE IN MY HEART P 521, $2.25
"Style brilliant . . . and suspenseful." —*San Francisco Chronicle*

THE PRIVATE WOUND P 531, $2.25
[Blake's] best novel in a dozen years . . . . An intensely penetrating study of sexual passion. . . . A powerful story of murder and its aftermath."
—Anthony Boucher, *The New York Times*

A QUESTION OF PROOF P 494, $1.95
"The characters in this story are unusually well drawn, and the suspense is well sustained." —*The New York Times*

THE SAD VARIETY P 495, $2.25
"It is a stunner. I read it instead of eating, instead of sleeping."
—Dorothy Salisbury Davis

THERE'S TROUBLE BREWING P 569, $3.37
"Nigel Strangeways is a puzzling mixture of simplicity and penetration, but all the more real for that." —*The Times Literary Supplement*

THOU SHELL OF DEATH   P 428, \$1.95
"It has all the virtues of culture, intelligence and sensibility that the most exacting connoisseur could ask of detective fiction."
                    —*The Times* [London] *Literary Supplement*

THE WIDOW'S CRUISE   P 399, \$2.25
"A stirring suspense. . . . The thrilling tale leaves nothing to be desired."
                    —*Springfield Republican*

THE WORM OF DEATH   P 400, \$2.25
"It [The Worm of Death] is one of Blake's very best—and his best is better than almost anyone's."   —Louis Untermeyer

John & Emery Bonett

A BANNER FOR PEGASUS   P 554, \$2.40
"A gem! Beautifully plotted and set. . . . Not only is the murder adroit and deserved, and the detection competent, but the love story is charming."   —Jacques Barzun and Wendell Hertig Taylor

DEAD LION   P 563, \$2.40
"A clever plot, authentic background and interesting characters highly recommended this one."   —*New Republic*

Christianna Brand

GREEN FOR DANGER   P 551, \$2.50
"You have to reach for the greatest of Great Names (Christie, Carr, Queen . . .) to find Brand's rivals in the devious subtleties of the trade."
                    —Anthony Boucher

TOUR DE FORCE   P 572, \$2.40
"Complete with traps for the over-ingenious, a double-reverse surprise ending and a key clue planted so fairly and obviously that you completely overlook it. If that's your idea of perfect entertainment, then seize at once upon *Tour de Force.*"   —Anthony Boucher, *The New York Times*

James Byrom

OR BE HE DEAD   P 585, \$2.84
"A very original tale . . . Well written and steadily entertaining."
                    —Jacques Barzun & Wendell Hertig Taylor, *A Catalogue of Crime*

Henry Calvin

IT'S DIFFERENT ABROAD   P 640, $2.84

"What is remarkable and delightful, Mr. Calvin imparts a flavor of satire to what he renovates and compels us to take straight."

—Jacques Barzun

Marjorie Carleton

VANISHED   P 559, $2.40

"Exceptional . . . a minor triumph."
—Jacques Barzun and Wendell Hertig Taylor, *A Catalogue of Crime*

George Harmon Coxe

MURDER WITH PICTURES   P 527, $2.25

"[Coxe] has hit the bull's-eye with his first shot."

—*The New York Times*

Edmund Crispin

BURIED FOR PLEASURE   P 506, $2.50

"Absolute and unalloyed delight."

—Anthony Boucher, *The New York Times*

Lionel Davidson

THE MENORAH MEN   P 592, $2.84

"Of his fellow thriller writers, only John Le Carré shows the same instinct for the viscera."   —*Chicago Tribune*

NIGHT OF WENCESLAS   P 595, $2.84

"A most ingenious thriller, so enriched with style, wit, and a sense of serious comedy that it all but transcends its kind."

—*The New Yorker*

THE ROSE OF TIBET   P 593, $2.84

"I hadn't realized how much I missed the genuine Adventure story . . . until I read *The Rose of Tibet*."   —Graham Greene

D. M. Devine

MY BROTHER'S KILLER   P 558, $2.40

"A most enjoyable crime story which I enjoyed reading down to the last moment."   —Agatha Christie

Kenneth Fearing

THE BIG CLOCK
P 500, $1.95

"It will be some time before chill-hungry clients meet again so rare a compound of irony, satire, and icy-fingered narrative. *The Big Clock* is . . . a psychothriller you won't put down." —*Weekly Book Review*

Andrew Garve

THE ASHES OF LODA
P 430, $1.50

"Garve . . . embellishes a fine fast adventure story with a more credible picture of the U.S.S.R. than is offered in most thrillers."

—*The New York Times Book Review*

THE CUCKOO LINE AFFAIR
P 451, $1.95

". . . an agreeable and ingenious piece of work." —*The New Yorker*

A HERO FOR LEANDA
P 429, $1.50

"One can trust Mr. Garve to put a fresh twist to any situation, and the ending is really a lovely surprise." —*The Manchester Guardian*

MURDER THROUGH THE LOOKING GLASS
P 449, $1.95

". . . refreshingly out-of-the-way and enjoyable . . . highly recommended to all comers."

—*Saturday Review*

NO TEARS FOR HILDA
P 441, $1.95

"It starts fine and finishes finer. I got behind on breathing watching Max get not only his man but his woman, too."

—Rex Stout

THE RIDDLE OF SAMSON
P 450, $1.95

"The story is an excellent one, the people are quite likable, and the writing is superior." —*Springfield Republican*

Michael Gilbert

BLOOD AND JUDGMENT
P 446, $1.95

"Gilbert readers need scarcely be told that the characters all come alive at first sight, and that his surpassing talent for narration enhances any plot. . . . Don't miss."

—*San Francisco Chronicle*

THE BODY OF A GIRL
P 459, $1.95

"Does what a good mystery should do: open up into all kinds of ramifications, with untold menace behind the action. At the end, there is a bang-up climax, and it is a pleasure to see how skilfully Gilbert wraps everything up."

—*The New York Times Book Review*

THE DANGER WITHIN　　　　　　　　　P 448, $1.95

"Michael Gilbert has nicely combined some elements of the straight detective story with plenty of action, suspense, and adventure, to produce a superior thriller."　　　　　　　　　　—*Saturday Review*

FEAR TO TREAD　　　　　　　　　　　　P 458, $1.95

"Merits serious consideration as a work of art."

　　　　　　　　　　　　　　　　　—*The New York Times*

Joe Gores

HAMMETT　　　　　　　　　　　　　　P 631, $2.84

"Joe Gores at his very best. Terse, powerful writing—with the master, Dashiell Hammett, as the protagonist in a novel I think he would have been proud to call his own."　　　　　　　—*Robert Ludlum*

C. W. Grafton

BEYOND A REASONABLE DOUBT　　　　P 519, $1.95

"A very ingenious tale of murder . . . a brilliant and gripping narrative."
　　　　　　　　—*Jacques Barzun and Wendell Hertig Taylor*

THE RAT BEGAN TO GNAW THE ROPE　　P 639, $2.84

"Fast, humorous story with flashes of brilliance."

　　　　　　　　　　　　　　　　　—*The New Yorker*

Edward Grierson

THE SECOND MAN　　　　　　　　　　P 528, $2.25

"One of the best trial-testimony books to have come along in quite a while."　　　　　　　　　　　　　　—*The New Yorker*

Bruce Hamilton

TOO MUCH OF WATER　　　　　　　　P 635, $2.84

"A superb sea mystery. . . . The prose is excellent."
　—*Jacques Barzun and Wendell Hertig Taylor, A Catalogue of Crime*

Cyril Hare

DEATH IS NO SPORTSMAN　　　　　　P 555, $2.40

"You will be thrilled because it succeeds in placing an ingenious story in a new and refreshing setting. . . . The identity of the murderer is really a surprise."　　　　　　　　　　　　—*Daily Mirror*

DEATH WALKS THE WOODS   P 556, $2.40

"Here is a fine formal detective story, with a technically brilliant solution demanding the attention of all connoisseurs of construction."

—Anthony Boucher, *The New York Times Book Review*

AN ENGLISH MURDER   P 455, $2.50

"By a long shot, the best crime story I have read for a long time. Everything is traditional, but originality does not suffer. The setting is perfect. Full marks to Mr. Hare."   —*Irish Press*

SUICIDE EXCEPTED   P 636, $2.84

"Adroit in its manipulation . . . and distinguished by a plot-twister which I'll wager Christie wishes she'd thought of."

—*The New York Times*

TENANT FOR DEATH   P 570, $2.84

"The way in which an air of probability is combined both with clear, terse narrative and with a good deal of subtle suburban atmosphere, proves the extreme skill of the writer."   —*The Spectator*

TRAGEDY AT LAW   P 522, $2.25

"An extremely urbane and well-written detective story."

—*The New York Times*

UNTIMELY DEATH   P 514, $2.25

"The English detective story at its quiet best, meticulously underplayed, rich in perceivings of the droll human animal and ready at the last with a neat surprise which has been there all the while had we but wits to see it."   —*New York Herald Tribune Book Review*

THE WIND BLOWS DEATH   P 589, $2.84

"A plot compounded of musical knowledge, a Dickens allusion, and a subtle point in law is related with delightfully unobtrusive wit, warmth, and style."   —*The New York Times*

WITH A BARE BODKIN   P 523, $2.25

"One of the best detective stories published for a long time."

—*The Spectator*

Robert Harling

THE ENORMOUS SHADOW   P 545, $2.50

"In some ways the best spy story of the modern period. . . . The writing is terse and vivid . . . the ending full of action . . . altogether first-rate."

—Jacques Barzun and Wendell Hertig Taylor, *A Catalogue of Crime*

Matthew Head

THE CABINDA AFFAIR   P 541, $2.25
"An absorbing whodunit and a distinguished novel of atmosphere."
—Anthony Boucher, *The New York Times*

THE CONGO VENUS   P 597, $2.84
"Terrific. The dialogue is just plain wonderful."
—*The Boston Globe*

MURDER AT THE FLEA CLUB   P 542, $2.50
"The true delight is in Head's style, its limpid ease combined with humor
and an awesome precision of phrase."   —*San Francisco Chronicle*

M. V. Heberden

ENGAGED TO MURDER   P 533, $2.25
"Smooth plotting."   —*The New York Times*

James Hilton

WAS IT MURDER?   P 501, $1.95
"The story is well planned and well written."
—*The New York Times*

P. M. Hubbard

HIGH TIDE   P 571, $2.40
"A smooth elaboration of mounting horror and danger."
—*Library Journal*

Elspeth Huxley

THE AFRICAN POISON MURDERS   P 540, $2.25
"Obscure venom, manical mutilations, deadly bush fire, thrilling climax
compose major opus.... Top-flight."
—*Saturday Review of Literature*

MURDER ON SAFARI   P 587, $2.84
"Right now we'd call Mrs. Huxley a dangerous rival to Agatha Christie."
—*Books*

Francis Iles

BEFORE THE FACT   P 517, $2.50
"Not many 'serious' novelists have produced character studies to compare with Iles's internally terrifying portrait of the murderer in *Before the Fact,* his masterpiece and a work truly deserving the appellation of unique and beyond price."   —Howard Haycraft

MALICE AFORETHOUGHT   P 532, $1.95
"It is a long time since I have read anything so good as *Malice Aforethought,* with its cynical humour, acute criminology, plausible detail and rapid movement. It makes you hug yourself with pleasure."
      —H. C. Harwood, *Saturday Review*

Michael Innes

THE CASE OF THE JOURNEYING BOY   P 632, $3.12
"I could see no faults in it. There is no one to compare with him."
      —*Illustrated London News*

DEATH BY WATER   P 574, $2.40
"The amount of ironic social criticism and deft characterization of scenes and people would serve another author for six books."
      —Jacques Barzun and Wendell Hertig Taylor

HARE SITTING UP   P 590, $2.84
"There is hardly anyone (in mysteries or mainstream) more exquisitely literate, allusive and Jamesian—and hardly anyone with a firmer sense of melodramatic plot or a more vigorous gift of storytelling."
      —Anthony Boucher, *The New York Times*

THE LONG FAREWELL   P 575, $2.40
"A model of the deft, classic detective story, told in the most wittily diverting prose."   —*The New York Times*

THE MAN FROM THE SEA   P 591, $2.84
"The pace is brisk, the adventures exciting and excitingly told, and above all he keeps to the very end the interesting ambiguity of the man from the sea."   —*New Statesman*

THE SECRET VANGUARD   P 584, $2.84
"Innes . . . has mastered the art of swift, exciting and well-organized narrative."   —*The New York Times*

THE WEIGHT OF THE EVIDENCE   P 633, $2.84
"First-class puzzle, deftly solved. University background interesting and amusing."   —*Saturday Review of Literature*

Mary Kelly

THE SPOILT KILL P 565, $2.40
"Mary Kelly is a new Dorothy Sayers. . . . [An] exciting new novel."
—*Evening News*

Lange Lewis

THE BIRTHDAY MURDER P 518, $1.95
"Almost perfect in its playlike purity and delightful prose."
—Jacques Barzun and Wendell Hertig Taylor

Allan MacKinnon

HOUSE OF DARKNESS P 582, $2.84
"His best . . . a perfect compendium."
—Jacques Barzun & Wendell Hertig Taylor, *A Catalogue of Crime*

Arthur Maling

LUCKY DEVIL P 482, $1.95
"The plot unravels at a fast clip, the writing is breezy and Maling's approach is as fresh as today's stockmarket quotes."
—*Louisville Courier Journal*

RIPOFF P 483, $1.95
"A swiftly paced story of today's big business is larded with intrigue as a Ralph Nader-type investigates an insurance scandal and is soon on the run from a hired gun and his brother. . . . Engrossing and credible."
—*Booklist*

SCHROEDER'S GAME P 484, $1.95
"As the title indicates, this Schroeder is up to something, and the unravelling of his game is a diverting and sufficiently blood-soaked entertainment."
—*The New Yorker*

Austin Ripley

MINUTE MYSTERIES P 387, $2.50
More than one hundred of the world's shortest detective stories. Only one possible solution to each case!

Thomas Sterling

THE EVIL OF THE DAY P 529, $2.50
"Prose as witty and subtle as it is sharp and clear. . .characters unconventionally conceived and richly bodied forth . . . . In short, a novel to be treasured."
—Anthony Boucher, *The New York Times*

Julian Symons

THE BELTING INHERITANCE   P 468, $1.95
"A superb whodunit in the best tradition of the detective story."
　　　　　　　　　　　　　—August Derleth, *Madison Capital Times*

BLAND BEGINNING   P 469, $1.95
"Mr. Symons displays a deft storytelling skill, a quiet and literate wit, a nice feeling for character, and detectival ingenuity of a high order."
　　　　　　　　　　　　　—Anthony Boucher, *The New York Times*

BOGUE'S FORTUNE   P 481, $1.95
"There's a touch of the old sardonic humour, and more than a touch of style." 　　　　　　　　　　　　　　　　　　—*The Spectator*

THE BROKEN PENNY   P 480, $1.95
"The most exciting, astonishing and believable spy story to appear in years. 　　　—Anthony Boucher, *The New York Times Book Review*

THE COLOR OF MURDER   P 461, $1.95
"A singularly unostentatious and memorably brilliant detective story."
　　　　　　　　　　　—*New York Herald Tribune Book Review*

Dorothy Stockbridge Tillet
(John Stephen Strange)

THE MAN WHO KILLED FORTESCUE   P 536, $2.25
"Better than average." 　　　　　—*Saturday Review of Literature*

Simon Troy

THE ROAD TO RHUINE   P 583, $2.84
"Unusual and agreeably told." 　　　　　—*San Francisco Chronicle*

SWIFT TO ITS CLOSE   P 546, $2.40
"A nicely literate British mystery . . . the atmosphere and the plot are exceptionally well wrought, the dialogue excellent." 　　—*Best Sellers*

Henry Wade

THE DUKE OF YORK'S STEPS   P 588, $2.84
"A classic of the golden age."
　　—Jacques Barzun & Wendell Hertig Taylor, *A Catalogue of Crime*

A DYING FALL   P 543, $2.50
"One of those expert British suspense jobs . . . it crackles with undercurrents of blackmail, violent passion and murder. Topnotch in its class."
　　　　　　　　　　　　　　　　　　　　　　　—*Time*

Henry Wade (cont'd)

THE HANGING CAPTAIN   P 548, $2.50

"This is a detective story for connoisseurs, for those who value clear thinking and good writing above mere ingenuity and easy thrills."
—*Times Literary Supplement*

Hillary Waugh

LAST SEEN WEARING . . .   P 552, $2.40

"A brilliant tour de force."   —Julian Symons

THE MISSING MAN   P 553, $2.40

"The quiet detailed police work of Chief Fred C. Fellows, Stockford, Conn., is at its best in *The Missing Man* . . . one of the Chief's toughest cases and one of the best handled."
—Anthony Boucher, *The New York Times Book Review*

Henry Kitchell Webster

WHO IS THE NEXT?   P 539, $2.25

"A double murder, private-plane piloting, a neat impersonation, and a delicate courtship are adroitly combined by a writer who knows how to use the language."   —Jacques Barzun and Wendell Hertig Taylor

Anna Mary Wells

MURDERER'S CHOICE   P 534, $2.50

"Good writing, ample action, and excellent character work."
—*Saturday Review of Literature*

A TALENT FOR MURDER   P 535, $2.25

"The discovery of the villain is a decided shock."   —*Books*

Edward Young

THE FIFTH PASSENGER   P 544, $2.25

"Clever and adroit . . . excellent thriller . . ."   —*Library Journal*

If you enjoyed this book you'll want to know about
THE PERENNIAL LIBRARY MYSTERY SERIES
Buy them at your local bookstore or use this coupon for ordering:

Qty	P number	Price
___	___	___
___	___	___
___	___	___
___	___	___
___	___	___
___	___	___
___	___	___
___	___	___
___	___	___
___	___	___
___	___	___
___	___	___
___	___	___
___	___	___
___	___	___

	postage and handling charge	$1.00
___ book(s) @ $0.25		___
	TOTAL	

Prices contained in this coupon are Harper & Row invoice prices only.
They are subject to change without notice, and in no way reflect the prices at
which these books may be sold by other suppliers.

**HARPER & ROW, Mail Order Dept. #PMS, 10 East 53rd St., New
York, N.Y. 10022.**
Please send me the books I have checked above. I am enclosing $_____
which includes a postage and handling charge of $1.00 for the first book and
25¢ for each additional book. Send check or money order. No cash or
C.O.D.s please

Name_____

Address_____

City_____ State_____ Zip_____
Please allow 4 weeks for delivery. USA only. This offer expires 11/30/84.
Please add applicable sales tax.